SCANDAL 52

SCANDAL 52

Andy Arnold

TATE PUBLISHING
AND ENTERPRISES, LLC

Published by Tate Publishing & Enterprises, LLC
127 E. Trade Center Terrace | Mustang, Oklahoma 73064 USA
1.888.361.9473 | www.tatepublishing.com

Tate Publishing is committed to excellence in the publishing industry. The company reflects the philosophy established by the founders, based on Psalm 68:11,
"The Lord gave the word and great was the company of those who published it."

Book design copyright © 2014 by Tate Publishing, LLC. All rights reserved.
Cover design by Allen Jomoc
Interior design by Manolito Bastasa

Published in the United States of America

ISBN: 978-1-63268-878-1
Fiction / Mystery & Detective / General
14.10.24

Acknowledgements

Tate Publishing: For accepting and publishing my story.

My parents: For proofreading, assisting, and supporting me with my novel.

Sue Mola: For encouraging and inspiring me to pursue writing.

Pam Telleen, Brian Maag, Dan Hamstra, Russell Vitrano, Tom and Shawna Reidy, John and Barb Tschopp, and Joyce and Don Smit: For proofreading my story and providing constructive feedback.

Kathryn Makeever and Joe Picciuca: For consulting me about the characteristics of people with Asperger's syndrome.

Jim Even: For consulting me about school procedures.

1

"Mississippi," began Peter as he rapidly mangled the napkin stored in his pocket. His hands worked quickly as he rolled the napkin bits between his fingers at a breathtaking rate. Having a fidget was one of the best ways for eleven-year-old Peter Salmons to calm his nerves and ease the stress of being the center of attention. Spelling words in front of a panel of judges, his classmates, and a huge crowd was way more difficult than spelling words at home while practicing with Mom and Dad. Usually, Peter thrived at spelling, but this situation was causing so much anxiety!

"M-R-S…oh no, wait, let me try again," exclaimed Peter very rapidly. "Let me try again, please, I'm so sorry, so sorry, please, please!"

A light snicker rippled through the crowd, some from Peter's classmates who had often made fun of him through the years. *This sucks!* he thought. He would usually nail that word in his sleep, but he was so nervous. Mississippi was such an easy word but his mind just didn't want to work right now.

"It's okay," said spelling bee judge Norman Weber. "You are allowed to correct yourself one time during each round. Please try again."

ooooo

"Please God, please calm Peter's nerves," prayed Jennifer Salmons silently as she sat in the crowd next to her husband, Joe. She and Joe had spent numerous hours going over challenging words with their son to prepare him for the annual spelling bee. While Peter was a student at Centerville Intermediate School, she was a teacher aide at one of the other schools in District 52. She actually worked in the ROCKETS program, which was the program in the county's cooperative that serviced students with severe autism. ROCKETS stood for Realizing Our Creative Knowledge and Educational Targets Successfully; therefore, she was aware of several of the teaching strategies for students with disabilities. She had worked with Peter at home as had his young resource teacher at his school on spelling challenging words.

They had taught Peter various mnemonics, which are memory strategies for remembering information. One of the memory strategies for spelling Mississippi was "I travels all the way to Mississippi with no y." She had not taught Peter that mnemonic since Mississippi was a super easy word for him. In fact, he could spell better than most kids his age. His main issue was his social skills and feeling anxious being around people. This was a symptom of his Asperger's syndrome, which is a level of high-functioning autism. This struggle with being in front of a huge crowd was what was causing Peter to not be able to think clearly right now. Jennifer prayed that Peter could calm himself and do what they had practiced.

ooooo

Peter took a deep breath, which was a coping strategy he had learned in a social story read to him by his resource teacher, Ms. Jones, and his social worker, Mrs. Green. The social story had also reminded Peter to spell words slowly during the spelling bee. This was easier said than done! It was much harder to stay calm and spell words slowly in the heat of the moment than while practicing.

"Mississippi, M-I-S-S-I-S-S-I-P-P..." *I've got to think! What was that last letter?* There were so many people in the crowd. He saw Tommy, who had made fun of his hand flapping back in third grade. He forgot where his mom and dad were sitting because of all the people. He was so nervous, his mind was going a mile a minute, and the napkin in his pocket was now shredded in a gazillion pieces! *Deep breath,* he reminded himself.

One of his best friends, fifth-grade classmate Betsy Lindgren, made eye contact with him. She and one of his other best friends, Sammy Jones, often looked out for Peter and wanted the best for him. Although this was technically cheating, she made the motion of rubbing her eye.

"I!" shouted Peter excitedly.

"That is correct," said Mr. Weber with a hint of happiness in his own voice.

ooooo

Joe Salmons pumped his fist. How he loved his son dearly and would do anything for him. As an electrical engineer, he often dealt with numbers and figures. Peter's developmental struggles, especially in the early years, had frustrated him. Joe liked life to be orderly—when things worked out much as a mathematical formula. He and his wife had done everything by the book during her pregnancy and Peter's infancy years. Peter was supposed to live a normal life playing soccer, having lots of friends, etc. After counseling and self-examination, Joe had learned to love and accept Peter the way he was. Now, he knew with absolute certainty that he would not trade Peter for the most athletic, talented, and socially normal kid in the world.

ooooo

When Peter's turn came again, Mr. Weber said, "Rudimentary," in his typical monotone voice.

Once again, Peter's heart pounded in rapid succession. He actually had nailed the word on a spelling pretest a month ago. However, now his mind was going in a million different directions. *Rude*, he was thinking, that was an adjective, but did it apply to this bigger word? No, it didn't…oh, would everyone just stop staring at him? Peter quickly flapped his hands in the air. Oh, shoot, he was on stage! *Come on, take a deep breath!* "Rudimentary, R-U-D-I-M-E-N-T-R-E...oops, I'm sorry, can I try again? Please, Mr. judge, please!" "I'm sorry," said Mr. Weber. "You're only allowed one correction each round, sorry."

Peter was devastated! He shouted, "I need a sensory break!" He then ran out of the gymnasium and ran into the bathroom to get away from the crowd. Having this many people staring at him was like having his eyes closed and hearing balloons popping every few seconds.

ooooo

Jennifer pursed her lips. She too was greatly disappointed and felt like crying. How could this happen? These were the early rounds! She had seen Peter flap his hands momentarily. This was a behavior Peter often engaged in when he felt excited, frustrated, or nervous. She was not surprised that Peter needed a sensory break. Many kids with autism, including the students she worked with on a daily basis, felt over-stimulated and stressed when too much was going on. Peter's school and her school had sensory break rooms, which had calming tools such as weighted blankets, lava lamps, and squeeze machines. Right now, Peter was probably taking his sensory break in a restroom. Despite her sadness at Peter's failure, she would put on a good face during the reception as she hoped Joe would so that they could be a positive example for their only child.

In addition to her melancholy, she also felt disgust and frustration at the district and spelling bee committee. Peter, with his disability and his Individual Education Plan (IEP) that stated his need for extended time and other accommodations for assignments and tests, should have been allowed more chances to correct himself. She had actually taken that issue up with the spelling bee committee and Superintendent Andrew Steinbeck. However, in typical Steinbeck fashion, he had argued about the good of all the students and about real world equality. Although Jennifer saw where he was coming from, it was hard to take because Peter was her son. Also, as a paraprofessional in the ROCKETS program, the students she worked with were even less fortunate than Peter. If they were treated equally as other general education students, they would fail. Fair was definitely not equal, and her students would need accommodations and modifications for the rest of their lives. Kids with disabilities usually needed some bending of the rules in order to level the playing field, but Steinbeck didn't seem to understand that.

As the Salmons drove home, Peter kept saying over and over, "M-I-S-S-I-S-S-I-P-P-I, easy word, M-I-S-S-I-S-S-I-P-P-I, easy word, M-I-S-S-I-S-S-I-P-P-I, easy word, rudimentary, rudimentary, R-U-D-I-M-E-N-T-A-R-Y."

"Peter, it's okay," said Jennifer. "You tried and did the best you could."

"Yes, I tried, T-R-I-E-D. Mr. Judge had on red. I don't like red." Peter then flapped his hands as he thought about this. Ever since he was a child, he had not liked red. Jennifer figured it probably had to do with red traffic lights. Since red lights made cars stop, it disrupted Peter's routine and slowed down his process of getting from point A to B. That was the best guess that she, Joe, the therapists and doctors could come up with. One thing that amazed Jennifer was that the medical and education profession still knew so little about autism. There was still so much debate on what causes autism and how to teach and help kids with autism. In fact, in the ROCKETS program, teachers and the other professionals such as behavioral therapists, social workers, etc. were constantly disagreeing and changing their ideas of what everyone should be doing. This was maddening for Jennifer and the other aides, because they never knew what to do since their many bosses never seemed to know. The reason this ignorance most concerned Jennifer was because one out of one hundred boys are diagnosed with autism. With this alarming number, society had to be more knowledgeable on how to work with these kids.

2

Peter lay in bed crying that night. Why were so many things in life hard for him? Spelling was supposed to be his ticket to being cool. He could spell well because he often pictured words the way they were spelled. Sometimes, he even spelled words out loud when there was no specific reason to do so. That sometimes drove his mom and dad crazy, but they had learned over time that that was just the way he was.

However, with such a large audience, and several of them being students who had sometimes made fun of him, his mind just didn't work the way it usually did. Peter thought, *Five-year-olds can spell Mississippi. Why was that word so hard for me?* He should not have had so much trouble with that word. Thinking of five-year-olds made him reflect on an incident when he was five years old. His parents had been going through their nightly battle with him trying to get him to brush his teeth.

"Come on, Peter, we have to do this," said his dad in his gruff voice.

His mom was holding him while Dad moved the toothbrush back and forth against his teeth. It felt like sandpaper being forcefully shoved along his teeth!

"Now, Peter, first brush teeth, then glass of orange juice," said his mom in her soothing voice.

Even though he had felt slightly better by her words, the pain was still too much to take. He finally pulled his face away from his dad, who responded by slamming the toothbrush down.

"Peter, you need to grow up and act like a big boy. It's just toothpaste!"

"Honey," said Mom, "it may be only toothpaste to you, but to him, it's completely different!"

"Forget it then!" said a frustrated Joe as he stormed out of the bathroom. Even though Peter had trouble reading facial expressions, he could read tones very well. He had known his dad was mad at him, and this made Peter very sad about himself. Even now, Peter remembered almost word for word the conversation his parents had had in the bathroom that night. In addition to his excellent spelling, he had an excellent memory of specific quotes, even from years earlier. Sometimes these quotes were completely irrelevant. Remembering this particular conversation made Peter very sad, and he finally cried himself to sleep.

ooooo

The next day, which was a Saturday, Peter played with Betsy and his other best friend, Sammy. This made him feel better about his spelling bee failure the previous night. Sammy and Betsy were very patient with Peter despite his social mishaps, often trying to help Peter better fit in at school and also accepting him for the way he was. The three friends were currently playing an intense game involving every individual trying to score points by shooting each other with Nerf bullets. However, there was only one gun. The person with the gun had to find the others who were hiding. Those without the gun had to try to wrestle the gun away from the shooter.

Peter laughed as Sammy wrestled him to the ground in an effort to yank his toy gun away from him.

"I'm going to get that gun, you punk." Sammy playfully teased Peter while giving him a noogie.

Normally, Peter was not so comfortable with physical contact if it was someone he didn't know, but he didn't mind because Sammy was one of his best friends. Also, he liked noogies because they provided harder contact. While Sammy and Peter wrestled, Peter said in his best Mr. T voice, "I'm gonna bust you up."

Sammy, knowing that Peter loved quoting movies, asked, "What movie is that from?"

"It's from Rocky 3," answered Peter.

As they continued to wrestle, Sammy stated, "If you're going to quote Rocky, you should say 'Yo, Adrian!'"

Peter scolded Sammy for not using Rocky's actual voice and said, "It's 'Yo, Adrian, Adrian!'"

Sammy finally wrestled the gun away from Peter, and Peter playfully yelled and darted for cover.

"All right, where are you guys?" yelled Sammy as he hunted around the backyard for Peter and Betsy.

Betsy jumped out from behind some bushes and tried to wrestle the gun out of Sammy's hands. While having their tug of war with the gun, an opportunistic Peter jumped out from behind the trees and snatched the gun from his friends. Betsy and Sammy, having been taken by surprise, darted off before Peter had a chance to nail them.

"Hey, no fair!" yelled Peter, who threw the gun down. "I quit!"

As Peter ran inside his house, Betsy and Sammy began to run after him. Both knew very well about Peter's disability and were sensitive to his needs and emotions.

"I'll talk to him," said Betsy. Sammy acquiesced knowing that Betsy was very good at handling Peter when he became upset.

ooooo

Betsy walked up the stairs to Peter's bedroom. Peter often had these temper tantrums when he became frustrated. Even though she didn't always understand why Peter got so upset, she knew he was born that way. It always made her sad when other kids teased Peter. She knew that Peter was really very nice. One time at school a couple of years ago, Peter had become angry when several kids were talking about shooting birds. As she knocked and walked into Peter's bedroom, he was sitting in his room mumbling gibberish.

"Peter, is it okay if I come in and we talk?" said Betsy.

Peter didn't answer but he also did not object. He was taking deep breaths and calming himself down.

"Why are you upset?" asked Betsy.

"You guys ran too quickly," answered Peter.

"Bud, that's part of the game. You did an awesome job taking away the gun. I know you thought you were going to be able to shoot us quickly, but sometimes things don't work…"

"And that's okay," continued Peter. "Too bad I don't have a social story about playing this game. That would help."

"A social story? What's that?"

Peter responded in a very mechanical voice, "A social story is a story that describes a situation, skill, or concept in terms of relevant social cues, perspectives, and common responses in a specifically defined style and format. It helps kids on the autism spectrum cope with change, manage anger, and deal with specific situations such as going to McDonald's. Social stories should be in this order: one descriptive statement, one perspective statement, and one directive statement."

"Huh?" said Betsy.

Peter went on to outline the components of a social story with textbook precision, and Betsy resisted the urge to tell Peter she didn't need that much information. Betsy understood that Peter tended to explain things in too much detail and that this was just part of who he was. She was pretty confused about what a social story was since Peter explained it using many big words. Peter was not able to read Betsy's facial expression to see that she was not understanding his explanation. Oftentimes at school, when Peter would talk about trains or computers, other kids would get bored and would not be able to get in a word. They often would then just walk away, and Peter would sometimes keep talking when no one was there. As Betsy listened to Peter explain about social stories, she gathered that they basically help kids know how to act in certain situations.

"Wow, these stories sound pretty powerful. Do they work most of the time?"

"Yeah, they help me most of the time."

Peter showed Betsy some of the social stories that he had in a folder. Betsy saw some of the titles that included "What I Can Do If I Feel Angry," "How to Act in My Classroom," and "Keeping Myself Clean." Now, Betsy was beginning to understand what social stories were.

"One time, Mrs. Green read to me a social story about losing in a game." Peter then recited part of the story and what the story told him to do in the event that he lost in a game.

"I just forgot to use it."

"That's all right," said Betsy. "Just remember not to give up when you play a game and things don't work out. Keep playing hard. Now, let's go out there and try to get that gun away from Sammy!"

3

Peter was fidgeting with his koosh ball Sunday morning as he sat in the pew at Centerville Community Church while he listened to Reverend Pete Thompson's sermon. Peter enjoyed church, for this was a place where most people were friendly and he didn't feel belittled for being different. Most of the kids here were nice and did not make fun of him. However, he was disappointed that Betsy and Sammy attended different churches. Some of the stories of Christianity were hard for Peter to grasp, such as the stories of God being extra harsh in the Old Testament, but overall Peter liked what the church taught. He liked the fact that Jesus was so loving and wanted all people to love one another.

Today's sermon was about God wanting us all to go out and make disciples of all nations. Thompson was asserting that that did not necessarily mean that all people had to become missionaries. He claimed that in a sense, God gives all people chips. Thompson explained that these chips are not literal chips, but figurative ones. That helped Peter since he would have been confused. He certainly couldn't remember God ever giving him a bag of chips! Thompson went on to explain that these chips stood for good deeds. We could use these chips and give them to people to help make their days better. An example would be if we saw someone crying, we could give them a hug. Another example would be giving a compliment to someone saying that they look nice today. Even just saying hi to someone could help make their day a little better. Peter was still a little confused about the concept of these chips, but Reverend Thompson's concrete examples helped him understand better.

"That was…a good sermon," said Peter.

"Why, thank you, Peter," said Reverend Thompson. "I appreciate you being here and listening to my sermons. You're a good man."

Peter looked at his mom who mouthed, "Thank you."

"Thank you," said Peter. "You put on a different cologne today."

"I did?" Thompson laughed. "Wow, I wasn't even aware of that. I was in a bit of a hurry."

After Peter ran off, the pastor reflected on Peter's membership at the church. Peter had certainly brought much joy and happiness to everyone at the church. Even though he had his quirks and would sometimes need to leave the sanctuary because of too much going on, Peter had a great heart and was a blessing. At a young age, Peter would sometimes scream out and have to be taken out of the sanctuary by his parents, but his ability to sit through a whole sermon was definitely improving.

Thompson laughed inside as he remembered Jennifer showing him a while back a drawing that young Peter had made of the crucifixion of Jesus. The picture had shown Jesus hanging on the cross, the two robbers on their crosses, and then a helicopter hovering above the scene. Jennifer had said she asked Peter what the helicopter was and he had said that that was the pilot who had wanted to kill Jesus. Another time, Peter drew a picture of a wedding scene and he labeled the groom's men as husband's maids! Ah, yes, since Peter took things very literally, Jennifer had actually talked to him about trying to use very specific and concrete examples in his sermons. That was one of the reasons in today's sermon he had explained and gave specific examples of the good-deed chips. Although it was hard to modify all of his sermons, he tried to be sensitive to Peter's needs.

ooooo

As Peter and his parents left church, they stopped at the Food Planet restaurant for this was part of their typical Sunday routine. Peter ordered his customary grilled cheese sandwich with a side of cream of chicken soup. As they ate, they talked about church and Sunday School.

"What did Thompson mean by missionary?" asked Peter.

"A missionary is a person that goes around the world telling other people about Jesus and God," explained Jennifer.

"Why did he say 'not everyone has to be a missionary'? Aren't all Christians supposed to tell people about Jesus?"

"What Mr. Thompson was saying was that instead of everyone getting a job where they travel the world to tell people about Jesus, we can show Jesus's love by simply being nice to one another," explained Joe.

Jennifer marveled at Peter's innocence and being so inquisitive about his faith, even at eleven years of age. She would certainly not trade Peter for any kid in the world. In a way, having his disability was kind of a blessing. If Peter was a normal eleven-year-old, there would be a greater chance that he would not have such a childlike faith.

4

As Peter took his seat during Mr. Alonzo's social studies class, he nervously scanned the classroom. He wanted to make sure that Frank O'Day was not approaching him. This year, Peter was fortunate not to have Frank in his homeroom class, where he spent most of the day. He was extra glad not to have Frank for lunch. Although the kids at this school had most of their subjects with one teacher, the fifth graders were mixed up and rotated for social studies and math. Peter's stomach was always in knots when it was almost time to attend social studies.

Mr. Alonzo promptly began the lesson by doing the chapter review questions as a class. The first question was: What is an alluvial plain? Peter's hand flew up excitedly and, after being called on, he quoted the book word for word by saying that "an alluvial plain is a fan-shaped plain formed by sediments deposited by a river—"

"Very good, Peter—" began Mr. Alonzo.

Peter proceeded to talk in his rapid and mechanical voice. "Alluvial plains are typically found—

"Just the definition for now, Peter."

Several students laughed, and Mr. Alonzo scolded them.

Peter blushed. He just always got carried away and excited when he knew an answer. He often was able to remember definitions word for word and if he had had his way, he would have enjoyed spelling the word—Alluvial Plain, A-L-L-U-V-I-A-L-P-L-A-I-N. He was a little confused since Mr. Alonzo had asked, "What is an alluvial plain?" Therefore, he felt inclined to answer the whole question. If Mr. Alonzo had only asked, "What is the definition of an alluvial plain," he would have known what to have said. People were baffling.

As Peter left the classroom, Frank approached him in the hallway. He mimicked Peter's rapid speech and said, "Hey, Peter, can you tell me everything you know about alluvial plains?"

Peter, knowing that Frank really didn't want an answer, became very agitated and nervous. He lacked the social skills to make a clever comeback and said very rapidly, "Leave me alone, leave me alone, go away, I've got to get to math!"

Mimicking Peter's autism, Frank said again, "Oh, I'm sorry, you have fun at math. Don't forget your books." He then knocked the books out of Peter's hands.

Betsy and Sammy then came to his assistance.

"Frank, leave him alone, you jerk!" exclaimed Betsy. Sammy began helping Peter pick up his books, while Frank and his buddies snickered.

"Okay, Peter, you have fun with your boyfriend and girlfriend," said Frank.

"They're not my boyfriend and girlfriend!" whined Peter. "I'm only eleven and I—"

"Don't respond to them," reasoned Sammy. "They're trying to get a reaction out of you."

Just for kicks, Frank shoved Peter, who again responded by saying, "Stop, I'm going to be late for math. Go away, leave me alone." Peter then curled up on the floor and buried his hands in his face, not to cry but to distance himself from the hostile world.

"Oh, the baby is about to cry," said one of Frank's buddies as they began walking away.

Sammy stood up and was about to go after Frank, but Betsy restrained him. "Stop, you'll end up getting in bigger trouble. Let's help Peter get to math and then we can tell a teacher what happened."

∞∞∞

"Welcome, everyone," stated Adam Cruthers as he began the IEP (Individual Education Plan) annual review meeting for Peter. "The point of this meeting is to discuss Peter's progress from this past year and any educational concerns as well as to discuss goals for the next year. Let's begin by everyone here introducing themselves and signing the IEP form."

Mr. Cruthers was the assistant superintendent and possessed the role of Director of Special Services for District 52. The other members of Peter's IEP team—the speech pathologist, the occupational therapist, the nurse, social worker Mrs. Green, resource teacher Ms. Jones, and building principal Mrs. Mathers—all introduced themselves in standard fashion. Joe and Jennifer introduced themselves and signed the front page of the IEP form.

Jennifer was overall pleased with how the year was progressing so far. Even though she often had issues with the district, so far she thought things were going fairly well for Peter. His resource/inclusion teacher was a young first year teacher named Peggy Jones. Ms. Jones was an asset to the district because she was articulate, clear, compassionate, and very knowledgeable about special education. Although it was only October, Ms. Jones had succeeded so far in setting up Peter for success by pre-teaching certain lessons, modifying assignments and tests, and working with his other teachers to create a fairly predictable routine for him. Jennifer really appreciated the fact that Ms. Jones seemed to really understand that children with autism thrive on predictability.

"I think Peter has shown progress since the first few weeks of school with his adapting to change, but I definitely would like to continue working on that skill," explained Ms. Jones. She laid out what the goal was for Peter and what the process would look like for improving his skill of coping with change. "Another thing I've noticed about Peter, as have other teachers, is his exceptional ability to script information word-for-word. He'll often repeat entire paragraphs from textbooks word-for-word. However, he has difficulty explaining that information in his own words. That's another skill I'd like to work on with him during his resource time."

"Yeah," said Jennifer. "Sometimes, I'll try to have him help me cook. Peter can recite the recipe exactly, but he gets confused on what to do. One time when a direction told him to shake well before opening a can, he started shaking his body!"

Everyone at the meeting laughed, for most of them knew that Peter as well as many kids with Asperger's syndrome tend to interpret information very literally.

"Although we are proud of Peter's progress and his continued success with spelling, test taking, and memorization of facts, we are still concerned about his outbursts," stated Mrs. Mathers.

Leave it to Principal Mathers to ruin the positive tone of the meeting, thought Jennifer.

"Teachers have reported that Peter does continue to occasionally have meltdowns that manifest themselves in his screaming at the slightest unexpected noise and yelling and carrying on when his routine is disrupted. Just last week, he was on the floor kicking and screaming because his regular gym time was changed. He also will lose his temper and scream at classmates who antagonize him."

"First of all," exclaimed Jennifer, "I am aware of Peter's meltdowns. He has them at home too, and we are constantly working with him on that. Peter is taking a taurine tablet once a day and he has a casein- and gluten-free diet, which helps prevent the meltdowns. Secondly, here's my problem with one of your accusations. If other kids are picking on Peter, why is *Peter* getting blamed for having the problem?"

"Sometimes, students look for a reaction," said Mathers.

"This is why Ms. Jones and I will continue working with Peter on coping strategies and reading social stories with him," explained Mrs. Green, whom Jennifer sensed seemed mildly perturbed at Mrs. Mather's negativity. "I just wanted you to be informed of what was going on," stated Mathers.

As Jennifer left the meeting, she reflected on Peter's toddler years. Her eyes watered as she remembered the play groups she and other young moms organized as they sought to teach their children to play. Although Peter was not yet officially diagnosed with Asperger's syndrome at the time, his play skills were significantly behind those of his peers. Although the other toddlers often engaged in at least parallel play, which is where they play next to each other, Peter played away from them. He often played in his own corner and sorted cars by very specific functions. Sometimes, he sorted them by color, other times by size, or even by which cars had cracks. When other kids asked to play with him, Peter, not yet verbal, would yell out and often run away. He had had so much trouble even at such a young age of fitting in with peers. Unfortunately, although these play groups would hopefully help Peter improve socially, his social ability would probably be an area of difficulty all his life.

Jennifer sighed because so many doctors, therapists, teachers, and other professionals over the years had so many different pieces of advice for her. It was so maddening, because autism, especially Asperger's syndrome, was so new and much of the research on various methods was inconclusive. She and Joe often had to play doctor and teacher and wear so many hats over the years in order to help Peter develop.

5

John Marsch chuckled to himself. This was going to be the easiest robbery he had ever committed. Being able to enter the elementary administration building with an electronic key card, he had no need to use his lock-picking skills. In fact, sometimes in the past, he had had to hack into high security buildings' systems in order to gain entry. Marsch swiped his card under the electronic lock, and the device made the standard *beep* sound. Marsch scanned the building and analyzed its setup in case he needed to make a quick getaway.

He saw the superintendent's office straight ahead, the assistant superintendent's office next door, and a few other key offices. All the other desks, those of the less-important big wigs, were in the main area of the building. Now, he only needed to follow his client's advice on where in the building to find the desired equipment. Marsch was not sure why his client wanted to possess such expensive equipment, considering this individual was already considerably wealthy, but he didn't really care. He was simply paid to deliver the goods. Following his employer's directions to the tee, he finally located the Revolabs, the iPads, and the Smart Boards.

His client had specified how many of each item Marsch was supposed to take. He was confident that he and his friends had the means of stealing all the equipment, but his boss was clear about how much was desired. His partners, who were waiting outside, responded immediately when Marsch contacted them with his walkytalky. One of them rushed in to help him transport the heavy items, while the other kept watch outside. "Man, we might be able to keep this equipment and sell it ourselves," said the guy who was helping Marsch transport the boxes of Smart Boards.

"Don't even think about it," growled Marsch. "John Marsch is a man of his word. I promised the client that I would deliver the goods. When John Marsch makes a promise, he keeps it!"

"All right, don't pop a blood vessel, man. It was just an idea. Dude, man, did you forget to take a shower today?"

"Shut up, man," said Marsch. "I happen to like food with garlic. I had quite a bit of garlic tonight for dinner."

After ten more runs, the job was complete. As the men drove off in silence, Marsch sat quietly after another complete mission. After storing the cargo in his garage, he would contact his client and they would arrange when and how to transfer the stolen equipment. Marsch's client was very cautious and had rules about not being contacted at home. Usually the two of them liked to meet in a different town and in a private room so they would not risk being seen by a member of the community. For now, Marsch simply reflected on his life. He missed the thrill of battle, and being involved in slightly dangerous missions like this somewhat satisfied this need. Also, being involved in illegal behavior was his way of spiting the enemy of his life.

ooooo

"Hi, Ms. Jones," said Peter as he walked into her small resource room located on the second floor of Centerville Intermediate School. "You are wearing different makeup today. It smells differently, that's how I know."

"Wow, buddy, nothing gets past you."

Peter laughed because he could tell she was joking, but he was a little confused by that comment. He often took things very literally and got confused by figures of speech.

"I like the smell, but I don't like the red design on your shirt. I don't like red."

"I know, I know, Peter. Anyway, we are going to do something a little different today," said Ms. Jones as she pulled out a dry-erase board with an orange laminated circle on it. The orange signified that there was going to be a change. She wrote on the board the figures 1 and 2 and then turned to Peter and said, "First, we are going to write a social story together, then you may work on homework."

Peter, feeling slightly anxious by this change, said, "But I have lots of work to do!"

"This will only take five minutes. I'm even going to set the red timer so you know exactly how long this will take."

Peter did feel calmed because he knew he could look at the timer and know exactly how much time was left since he could see the red disappearing. Seeing the red disappearing was also good since he hated red. Peter always liked knowing how long something was going to last and what was coming next.

Ms. Jones went on and asked Peter about what had happened the previous day in an incident where some kids were involved in a mischievous activity and he got caught for going along with it. Peter recited the scene in a very detailed manner. Ms. Jones wrote down something on a paper and asked Peter to read what she had written.

"Sometimes, friends do things that are not right. They will get into trouble, and so will I, if I go along with them," Peter read.

"Very good, Peter. What do you think you should do or say if friends tell you to do something wrong?"

"I could say N-O, explain to them the consequences of their actions, and tell them they'll get grounded, lose their Xbox, watch no TV, and…"

"You could do that, or maybe just tell them that it's not cool to do what they're about to do and then walk away."

"Yeah, I guess I could do that."

After more writing, Peter read, "When they ask me to do something wrong, I can tell them 'That's not cool, and I'd rather not do that,' and then walk away. My friends may laugh at me, but this is okay." After finishing reading, Peter said, "Friends, F-R-I-E-N-D-S."

Just as the red from the timer disappeared, Mrs. Mathers came to the door and asked Ms. Jones to step outside. Ms. Jones quickly crossed out the social story activity written by the number one on the dry-erase board and told Peter he could begin his homework. After stepping outside, Mrs. Mathers said, "Something has happened. There has been a major robbery at the administration building. We lost numerous Smart Boards, Revolabs, and iPads."

"Oh, my gosh!"

"Yeah, right now it's a circus over there. For now, we are going to ask that the kids not be informed. We just think at this time that all staff should be notified."

6

Detective John Scagglione and his partner, Kim Madigan, made their way through the crime scene tape and the local media throng as they walked toward the District 52 building. Several reporters tried to stop them and ask questions, but John and Kim declined to comment at the present time. They were here for one reason—to solve a crime that would certainly disturb the community.

At twenty-eight, John Scagglione was a no-nonsense officer trying to establish a long career in the Centerville police department. Having grown up on the south side of Chicago, John was relatively familiar with the dark side of life. That toughness assisted him when he did have confrontations with criminals.

"What a circus," muttered John to Kim. "I never thought while I was at the academy that I'd be investigating a crime at an elementary school district. Well, as long as I don't have to interview any kids. Don't think I'd have the patience for that."

"Oh, come on, Mr. Old Grouch," chided Kim. "Kids aren't that bad. They are actually a lot smarter than people give them credit for."

"Yeah, they're smart at manipulating parents, and they know that whining enough will get them what they want," snickered John.

"Oh, someday you'll have a couple of kids that will make your heart grow several sizes." Kim knew that John was currently in an on again-off again relationship with a young lady named Liz. Kim was a mother of two and in her late thirties. She knew John was still fairly young, not ready for commitment and especially fatherhood.

Making their way inside the building, Kim and John were led to Supt. Andrew Steinbeck's office. Steinbeck was sitting next to another man in a suit.

"Hello, I'm Detective Kim Madigan and this is Detective John Scagglione," said Kim as she and John matter-of-factly shook the two men's hands.

"Thank you for coming out," said Steinbeck politely. "This is indeed very tragic for the district. Anyway, this is the assistant superintendent, Mr. Adam Cruthers."

Cruthers had a distant look as he shook hands with the officers.

"We just have a few questions, and then we need to begin investigating the crime scene," said John. "First of all, we need an official statement about what happened and what was stolen."

"Half a shipment of Revolabs, which are classroom wireless amplification systems, half a shipment of iPads and a shipment of Smart Boards for several of the schools were stolen," said Steinbeck.

"How were these items noticed to be missing?" asked Kim.

"My administrative assistant Mrs. Sheila Van Order was the first to arrive at the office," explained Steinbeck. "While she was making copies, she noticed that half the district's new Smart Boards were missing. From what she told me, she then began searching to see if anything else was missing. Half an hour later, she then noticed that several of the newly purchased amplification systems and the newest versions of iPads were also missing."

"All right," said John as he continued taking notes and made eye contact with Kim before continuing. "We'll want to get a statement from Mrs. Van Order."

John was curious as to why Mrs. Van Order had not called the police sooner to at least report the missing Smart Boards. He sensed Kim felt the same way.

"One of the things I'm most curious about is why the thieves left half of all these items. That's kind of strange."

"Well, keep in mind," said Steinbeck, "that would have taken more time and manpower to transport that many more items." Steinbeck shook his head and looked sad. "This collection of technology was to completely modernize our district. In order to keep our kids competitive in a struggling economy, we would like our kids to have the best education possible. Our district had a timeline for ensuring that all our classrooms in all five schools would have one Smart Board in three years. This robbery puts us back several years!"

John continued, "From what we've heard through the preliminary report, there was no sign of forced entry. Therefore, whoever stole the equipment breached your security system. How could that have happened?"

"How can we know?" snapped Mr. Cruthers. "That's your job to find that out!"

As John glared at this assistant administrator, Kim interjected, "What we're trying to ask is if we should be suspicious of someone working inside the district stealing the equipment. Is there an electronic log of who entered the facility and when?"

"There is, and we have already checked it," answered Mr. Steinbeck very quickly. "The log states that one of my top administrative assistants was in the building at two in the morning, but we know it could not have been her."

John and Kim both stared at Steinbeck with wide eyes that begged him to elaborate.

"Pat Allen had her key card stolen from her purse three days ago at a district party at Anne's Pizzeria. She doesn't need to use her card normally during normal business hours to enter the district headquarters."

"Why didn't any of you cancel her key card?" asked Scagglione.

"We've been very busy and did not anticipate it being used for a robbery. I personally thought it was just some punk looking to cause trouble and perhaps who thought he was stealing a credit card. Even though we had a room in the restaurant just for district employees, we were not the only people in the building. I deeply regret my folly."

"All right," conceded Kim. "Still, even though this purse robbery occurred in a public facility, it still could have been another administrator or staff member that stole the card and used it to commit this robbery."

"First of all, we're one of the top districts in the state," grumbled Cruthers. "Our employees are thoroughly screened and given background checks..."

"At this time," said Steinbeck while motioning with his hand for Cruthers to back off and let him do the talking, "I have no reason to suspect that one of our employees committed this crime. I have the highest level of respect for all our teachers and administrators. I just know that no one here would have done this. Nonetheless, we will fully cooperate with the police to solve this."

"We appreciate your cooperation," said John. "We will need a copy of all your human resource files to see if anyone has anything in their background that we should be suspicious of."

"Why should we provide you with human resource files?" grumbled Cruthers. "That makes no sense! You have access to criminal information from your databases! Heck, we go to *you* for information about criminal backgrounds when we hire a new employee!"

Struggling to maintain his composure, John stated, "We do have criminal databases and we could find out if any of your employees have backgrounds. However, it will save us time if we look at your human resource files. Plus, I am not only interested if anyone has a criminal background. I want to know the big picture about everyone, where they've worked in the past, past evaluations at the school district, any clues about their history that may give us reason to be suspicious about them!"

In what was now sounding like a playground argument, Cruthers added, "Well, giving you the human resource files violates privacy laws and goes against our district policy."

"Right now," stated Steinbeck, becoming slightly more agitated, "I'm not concerned about legality and protocol. If providing the police with HR files will assist in the investigation, save the police time and help quickly bring the responsible persons to justice, so be it!"

John couldn't help but smirk at Cruthers. It was refreshing that at least the superintendent understood his position and was being helpful.

Cruthers froze up, clearly frustrated by his boss's decision.

ooooo

John and Kim methodically dusted for prints, retraced the criminals' steps, and got statements from Mrs. Van Order, Mrs. Allen and several other administrators. Mrs. Van Order spoke nervously and averted eye contact on several occasions when they interviewed her. When asked why she took so long to call the police, she explained, "I was totally shaken to find district property missing! First of all, I wanted to see what had been taken and be sure that a crime had indeed been committed. If there was a logical explanation, I didn't want to make a fool of myself and the district by calling the cops."

John and Kim then interviewed Mrs. Allen, who was responsible for the purchasing of school equipment and finance. She was very friendly and helpful but deeply distraught that her electronic key card was used by the thieves to enter the building. "No one ever thinks that they can be robbed. I left my purse for two minutes at my table and that is when it must have been stolen. I noticed it was missing the next evening when I rummaged through my purse to find my car keys! I feel so bad!" She was nonetheless helpful and provided information about the purchase date and the companies that sold the equipment and gave invoices to John and Kim.

"Did you notice anything unusual when you entered the building, other than the missing equipment? Was anything else out of place or did you hear anything?" asked Kim.

"Well, now that you mention it, the only thing that struck me as strange was that the building reeked of garlic when I entered. I was the second person to enter the building after Mrs. Van Order and I don't think she ever eats anything with garlic."

"Interesting," said John. "Nobody else mentioned the garlic smell."

ooooo

John and Kim then headed out of the administrative building with their notes and the human resource files. After making a statement to the media, the two cops got in their car and tried to figure the best course of action to take. Kim sighed and realized that the tedious process of reviewing the files of the employees, going over and over them, and interviewing more people would begin. What so many cop shows portrayed about detective work and the general public perception was not always accurate. Solving mysteries took lots of time and was often boring. Detectives had to review notes, details, and information over and over again for hours in order to find a link or useful clue.

"Well, I guess we'd better begin by talking to all the neighbors along the street and see if anyone noticed anything suspicious," began John.

"Yeah, the only problem is if the robbery occurred in the middle of the night, chances are slim anyone saw anything. But you're right, we do need to begin with that."

"I wonder what we should make of the garlic observation," said John.

"I'm not sure, but let's remember it. Even though it seems unimportant, it may be a useful clue. Any other thoughts?" asked Kim. "Do we consider Mrs. Allen the prime suspect?"

"I don't think so. For now, just a person of interest. I'm a pretty good judge of character and did not sense any red flags when speaking with Mrs. Allen. I didn't like that Cruthers character. Besides being a jerk, he seemed paranoid like he was trying to hide something."

"Yeah," agreed Kim, "but I also got a bad vibe about the superintendent. His answers kind of seemed staged, almost like he had it all planned out. He probably said the same things in his press statement." Kim sighed. "But maybe I just don't trust politicians, or in Steinbeck's case, an un-elected government employee in a high position."

"Right now, I'm very sure someone from the district is surely behind this crime," said John. "It would have been difficult and improbable for someone not connected with the district to have entered the room rented by the district at the pizza restaurant and then sneak into the exact purse of an administrator for the key card. Mrs. Allen may be our thief. She may have staged the purse robbery to deflect suspicion from herself. However, my gut is telling me that someone else from the district stole the card, then hired a thief to gain entry into the building and steal the equipment. My instinct is also telling me that this is going to be one of my most unusual cases ever."

7

Joe, Jennifer, and Peter watched the ten o'clock news, which was their typical ritual before going to bed. Peter had had his Special Olympics basketball practice after school. After coming home from practice, he continued with his routine of eating dinner, doing his homework, and then playing on his Xbox. Peter often became agitated and upset if his nightly routine, or any routine, was disrupted. He often would need a social story or warning in advance about his routine changing.

The news tonight ran the story of the robbery in the District 52 administration building. The anchor went over the facts of the case—what was stolen and what the dollar value of the items were. They interviewed the male and female detectives assigned to the case. The male detective, John Scagglione, said that "we will investigate all leads and not rest until the case is solved and the criminals are brought to justice." Next, there was a sound bite of the superintendent saying, "At the district office, we are deeply troubled by the theft. We are most troubled by the fact that the police do not have any leads or idea after searching the crime scene as to who the perpetrator is. I would like to ensure the taxpayers of this community that District 52 will fully cooperate with the local police to get to the bottom of this tragedy."

"Mom and Dad, he's not troubled. He is not one bit sad about what happened."

Jennifer smiled. Although her son was very poor at reading facial expressions, he was extraordinary at reading emotions through vocal tones. Whenever she or Joe gave Peter an angry look, he seemed to have no idea what was going on. However, whenever their tone of voice changed, he knew he was in trouble. Every time the two of them would try to hide their emotions with their voices, Peter was not fooled. This unique perception was not known to be typical with all kids with autism, at least not to Jennifer's knowledge. Peter's gifted perception of voice tones seemed to be his natural and special gift. Peter's assessment of Steinbeck basically matched Jennifer's, who always perceived the man as being someone who tried to portray himself as being so wonderful, but seemed like he looked out more for people he liked. Perhaps, Steinbeck was not upset about the robbery but more excited about an opportunity to create a positive self-image of himself on television.

"Who stole the stuff?" asked Peter.

"No one knows yet," explained Joe. "The police are trying to find out."

"That's right," said Peter. "They will 'not rest until the case is solved and the criminals are brought to justice,'" said Peter, mimicking Detective John Scagglione's voice.

Joe and Jennifer both laughed.

ooooo

During the next several days, Superintendent Andrew Steinbeck visited the different schools to meet with groups of students to answer any questions regarding the theft and what the district was going to do about it. Steinbeck visited Peter's math class and answered several questions the students had. Questions included: Are the criminals dangerous? Will they come back? Are our schools (kids) safe? What will the school do to keep this from happening again? Steinbeck at one point mentioned that the police were pursuing several leads. Peter suddenly raised his hand.

"Yes, Peter," said Steinbeck.

"You said on the news, 'We are most troubled by the fact that the police do not have any leads or idea after searching the crime scene as to who the perpetrator is.' But now you are saying, 'The police are pursuing several leads.'"

"Now, Peter, please do not talk that way to Dr. Steinbeck," said his math teacher.

"It's okay," said Steinbeck. "I'm pleased to see that you are following the news and asking lots of questions. A few days ago, the police did not have any leads. In the last few days, the police have been finding leads and pursuing them."

Peter shuttered. Had he done something wrong? He was nervous because he always felt like he was supposed to follow rules. He often followed rules very literally and to the letter. One of the general unwritten rules at school was to listen carefully and ask lots of questions. This "hidden curriculum" rule had been explained to him by various special education teachers over the years. Had he broken an unwritten rule without knowing? Oftentimes he got in trouble and didn't know what he had done wrong.

One such time occurred when he was still in the ROCKETS program for students with severe autism. At that time, Peter still had very limited vocabulary and could say only a few phrases. He and another student named Dan, a student who could only communicate in grunts and groans, were playing a game called "Don't Tip the Waiter" with Mr. Ian, the speech teacher. This game involved a one-foot cardboard waiter and placing bits of cardboard food on each side of the waiter without tipping him over. Dan had accidentally knocked over the waiter with his hands and had ruined the game. Mr. Ian had said in a playful tone, "What happened?" Peter knew from his voice that he was not angry. Therefore, Peter had wanted the same reaction. So, during the next game, while the waiter's trays were full of food, Peter socked the waiter just so he could get the positive reaction from Mr. Ian. However, Mr. Ian jumped up, picked up Peter, and sat him in the corner for his actions. Peter was so confused, because Mr. Ian had not reacted to him as he had to Dan for the exact same behavior. People truly confused Peter and he could never figure them out.

Once again in the present situation, Peter thought he was doing the right thing by thinking critically and asking questions. However, the math teacher became upset with his question. He just couldn't win sometimes.

8

John sipped on his coffee for his morning caffeine rush as he walked into the Centerville police department. He said his usual greeting to the desk receptionist, Christine Jensen. She was polite but was a fairly quiet and reserved person. He filled up his coffee and was heading toward his office when he ran into Allan Huisenga.

"Quite a case you're on!" said Huisenga.

"Yes indeed," agreed Scagglione. "Who would want to take so much expensive equipment from a school district?"

"People these days will do anything for an extra buck," said Allan. "Someone is probably going to try and sell the equipment for a profit."

"Yeah, but at the expense of a bunch of kids' education."

"I wish I was involved with this case," continued Huisenga. "I'm not sure if Chief Emanuel is up to the challenge of helping you solve this crime. There have been so many cases where he has made decisions that have hindered us from solving crimes. Ah, don't get me started. Good luck and find the jerks who did this. Let me know if you need any input."

John nodded as he went on his way to his office to continue his coffee and plan his day. He sipped his drink, relieved that he didn't have to listen to Allan Huisenga continue on for several more minutes of griping about Chief Emanuel. Huisenga had joined the force thirty years ago and felt that he deserved to be the chief. In truth, John knew that Huisenga was completely bitter about being passed over for the job. Huisenga had often whined about having paid his dues and deserving to be chief. He had complained a while back to John and Christine Jensen that Emanuel had gotten the job by "playing politics and kissing up to the former chief." He had gone on to gripe that "just because I don't kiss butts the way he does doesn't mean I shouldn't be chief. I know about crime control better than he does. He wouldn't know crime control if it jumped up and bit him in the you-know-what!"

John blocked Huisenga out of his mind by pulling out the first of many HR files to begin reviewing about the employees of District 52. Even though Kim had half the copies, this was going to take a lot of time. He would take about two hours of doing this and then take time investigating other cases.

ooooo

Jennifer sat with Mark in her workstation, which was called Green Work. Mark was six years old and had a severe level of autism. Jennifer was in charge of the Green workstation, which involved math. The kids in the ROCKETS program rotated to various work stations throughout the day in their classrooms. In each station, either the teacher or an aide would run that station and work with whichever child they had one-on-one with various goals. Jennifer showed Mark his countdown strip and said to him, "It's time to count, then reward." Jennifer knew that with kids with autism, it was very important to talk to them in as few words as possible. Too many words overwhelmed them and would cause them anxiety. Mark counted to eleven and Jennifer recorded in his binder "1–11." Just then, Ms. Anderson, the young teacher in her early twenties, walked over and saw what Jennifer had written.

"I'm actually going to ask that you write *what you did* to help him count to what he counted to. What you wrote doesn't tell me anything," Ms. Anderson said.

Jennifer complied with this directive but was confused. In order to monitor the progress of this student, all Ms. Anderson should need to know is how high the kid counted. Nonetheless, Jennifer took this in stride and promised to do what the teacher wanted. However, later in the day, Ms. Anderson actually gave Jennifer a data sheet with various sections with the numbers 1–100. She then asked Jennifer that each day, she have Mark count and then simply circle the number that he counted to. There was no need to provide any additional information.

Jennifer said, "This is fine, but this is exactly what I was doing before, and you said it didn't tell you anything."

Ms. Anderson looked a little put off, but Jennifer walked away and continued doing her daily duties. This had been a long day not only because of Ms. Anderson's behavior, but because Jennifer had to continue listening in the lounge about the gossip and rumors of the robberies. One aide had said, "Well, there goes the raise we were supposed to get. The district was going to give us a raise, but it will instead replace the equipment!" An aide from the ROCKETS program remarked, "Our classrooms in the ROCKETS program were each actually supposed to get a Smart Board. Now that half of them were stolen, we certainly won't get any of the leftovers. The district always treats us like our kids don't matter, and we're low on the priority list!" The staff went on to talk about various rumors leaked such as that it may have been an administrator who stole the equipment. The staff had already begun talking about who might have been behind it. Jennifer didn't want to hear this until they had more conclusive evidence.

Despite her rough day and occasional issues with her various superiors, Jennifer certainly did enjoy working in this program. She had many memories and experiences with many students. There was one student named Joey who had an obsession with going up to the classroom schedule, which consisted of sentence strips for each daily activity and tugging on the various strips. The teacher and the behavioral therapist had devised sentence strips specifically for Joey to tug when he felt the need to do so. Another student named Jibari had an obsession with tapping items such as pencils, puzzle pieces, crayons, etc. Again, the powers-that-be had instituted a behavior plan of having Jibari have a tapping box with various items to tap. When he felt the need to tap, he would have to signal the appropriate staff person with a picture card, and then he would have three minutes to use the tapping box. Jennifer's only problem was that when she had suggested a similar plan, the decision makers had blown off her idea. Oftentimes, teachers and therapists in the district and cooperative only liked an idea if it was their own. Many of the teachers in this program also seemed to have favorite aides, which Jennifer liked to call co-teachers. If a "co-teacher" came up with an idea, the teacher often would go with their idea.

Although these students were often in their own worlds, they could be very affectionate, lovable, and amazing. Jennifer truly did learn something every day from these kids. The student named Joey often loved to touch staff in the face to show his affection. Derrek would often say hi to staff, but he sometimes would say hi over and over again. Jenna was a cute little girl who would often say to Jennifer, "what are we doing today?" when she went to Jennifer's workstation. A little boy named Benny, who often ran in circles and did have some anger issues, just loved playing with letters. He would often arrange the letters to spell credits for movies and would arrange those credits exactly as they appeared at the ends of movies. Yes, these kids were definitely amazing and wonderful. The only issue in this program was often the staff and their egos.

9

John Scagglione stayed up late the second night in a row going over the HR files of the district employees. He reviewed the records of several teachers, aides, support staff, and administration, finding very little useful information. He switched between reading the HR files and running various names of district employees through the police department's criminal database from his home computer.

While talking to Liz earlier on his cell phone, she had admonished him "not to burn yourself out over this case." However, this was simply John's nature. He typically put all of his energy into his work until he solved a case. Having witnessed gang violence as a kid, he had a personal vendetta against the "bad guys." Also, this case was becoming more important to him after the first few days. Even though he was not always crazy about kids, there just seemed to be something completely evil about committing a crime that dealt with children. Even though the robbers had stolen from the administrative building, stealing from a school district was like taking from children. That made John very angry and more determined to solve the case.

After typing several names through the criminal database, he finally found something! He knocked over his half-empty can of Pepsi that he was drinking to get his caffeine fix. His black lab, Max, rushed over and began lapping up the soda waste. John fumbled with his cell phone as he speed-dialed Kim's number. Even though it was after midnight, he knew she kept her phone on vibrate in case he needed to contact her.

"What's going on?" asked a sleepy Kim.

"Listen to this. Anne Mathers, the principal at Centerville Intermediate School, pled guilty while in college to guess what."

"You got me buddy."

"Robbery."

"You don't say," remarked Kim, more awake now and carrying her phone out of her bedroom into her home office. "What did she plead guilty to?"

"She stole a television from an electronics store."

∞∞∞∞

A part of Jennifer wanted to cheer at hearing about Peter putting Steinbeck on the spot like he had. The math teacher had called her after school. Nonetheless, even though it was good to be a critical thinker, sometimes Peter's direct honesty got him into trouble. In fact, when the principal of his school, Mrs. Mathers, had made a comment a while back about always looking out for the best interest of the kids, Peter had not believed her. He had told Jennifer that Mrs. Mathers did not mean what she had said. Could there be something here? Or did Peter tend to overanalyze people's voices? Unfortunately, Jennifer did not trust many of the people in the district, or in the cooperative that serviced the ROCKETS program. This often stressed her out, even in her aide's job, because she worried so much for the kids. In fact, she just didn't see eye-to-eye with the district or cooperative on many things.

On her first evaluation as an aide this year, Ms. Anderson had mentioned that Jennifer seemed overly concerned about safety. Why should that be a problem? Being concerned for the safety of students is absolutely necessary in special education. One of her students was an adorable child named Derrick who had severe peanut allergies. Last year's teacher had initially said he could not eat in the cafeteria with the other students. Then they started telling other students and staff not to bring or eat anything with peanuts. However, Ms. Anderson had no problem this year with exposing tiny Derrick to other people with peanuts. Jennifer had brought up this issue with the young teacher, but Ms. Anderson just said that his allergies weren't as bad as his mom said they were. Ms. Anderson simply didn't seem concerned with it. Jennifer truly worried about Derrick having an allergic reaction and having to be rushed to the hospital! Now, Jennifer was being made out to be the bad guy by being overly cautious.

ooooo

As John and Kim entered Mrs. Mather's office at Centerville Intermediate School, she coldly let them in.

"Listen, officers," began Mathers. "I appreciate you trying to solve this crime, but I'm very busy. Unless you have some exceptionally important information, I have nothing more I can tell you. I've already made my statement, which isn't much information since I did not attend the district party and don't work at the administration building."

"Perhaps you can explain this," said John, tossing her file on her desk with the part about the college robbery highlighted.

Her face temporarily paled, but then she regained her composure. "I see. Well, you've got me. I've definitely made some mistakes throughout my life, mistakes that I'm not proud of. I was a college brat who needed money, so I hoped to be able to sell the television in order to make money. I assure you, as I have every employer in the education field, I have completely turned my life around. As a parent of two children, I'm looking to raise them with good values."

"I appreciate your story," said John. "However, it is quite a coincidence that you committed a robbery, which has now also occurred in your place of employment. Personally, I don't really believe in coincidences."

"What we're trying to say," said Kim, "is that we need to pursue all leads. We just need to let you know that you are a person of interest in this case."

"I guess I understand where you're coming from," said a resigned Mathers. "However, please don't waste too much time on me. You can check my phone records and interview anyone in my circle of friends. It would be better if you spend more time trying to find the real people responsible for this crime."

ooooo

As Peter and his mom walked through the grocery store, Peter tried to shield the lights from his eyes. Fluorescent lights often overstimulated him and sometimes triggered meltdowns. At Centerville Intermediate School, Ms. Jones had made sure that all his classes had lights that were covered. This made Peter much more comfortable in this new school. His mom took him to the grocery store once a week because she said it was a good way for him to learn social skills. He would often give the coupons to the cashier, pay the money, and answer any questions the cashier had. As a younger boy, Peter had had a very difficult time in the grocery store. This was often a setting that caused him severe meltdowns, and he also would often push groceries on the shelves away. This was very difficult on Mom.

Today, as they waited in line, he saw a lady whom he recognized waiting behind them.

"You look very familiar," said Peter in his rapid voice. Peter's eyes rolled into his head as the wheels were clearly turning, and he said, "Oh, you're Mrs. Van Order, a secretary at the administration building. Administration, A-D-M-I-N-I-S-T-R-A-T-I-O-N."

"Oh, hello," Mrs. Van Order said. "You look very familiar too. You must be a student at one of the schools."

"Hi," said Jennifer. "I think Peter might have seen you when his class took a tour of the administration building a few years ago. He never forgets a face."

"Yeah, you were wearing red. I don't like red," said Peter.

The two women chuckled.

"Well, anyway, I am Jennifer, Peter's mom. It is nice to meet you."

"Yeah, it's nice to meet you too," said Mrs. Van Order.

As they continued waiting in line, Peter tried to stay calm amidst all the many shoppers. He remembered her red outfit and winced since he could not stand the color red. As Peter and his mom talked to Mrs. Van Order, she seemed nervous. Peter also sensed that she was not sincere when she said "nice to meet you."

ooooo

John and Kim met in Police Chief Omar Emanuel's office for a debriefing on the case. Emanuel began by explaining, "The mayor has been giving me constant pressure to get to the bottom of this. This is certainly a public relations nightmare!"

"We're pursuing several leads," said Kim. "Right now, we believe someone from the district surely had to be behind this crime. The only employee who has any kind of criminal record is Mrs. Mathers, the principal from Centerville Intermediate School."

"Yeah, she seemed very defensive when we questioned her today," said John.

"Well, she probably did not like how it looked to have the principal questioned," said Emanuel, playing the devil's advocate.

"Or she just doesn't like cops, period," said Kim.

They went on to explain about her college crime, which Emanuel had to admit was pretty coincidental.

"As for the other administrative suspects," began John, "Dr. Steinbeck had nothing fishy on his record. Mr. Cruthers had a few DUIs back in his early days. The only thing strange about Mrs. Van Order, who averted our eye contact and waited a while to call the police, was that she was a secretary at an electronics store and was forced to resign. She also resigned from a former school district. An evaluation several years earlier indicated that she tends to not always be completely truthful."

"What about the lady whose card was stolen and used to enter the building?"

"Oh, you mean Mrs. Allen," said John. "She also had a clean record, plus, she seemed like a saint. I don't see her being a criminal."

"Well, keep in mind," said Kim, "sometimes criminals can be very good actors and seem like good people. She may be a wolf in sheep's clothing."

"Well, this is definitely interesting stuff," said Emanuel. "However, there still isn't much to go on here. Keep working and let's try to get to the bottom of this soon! This crime not only makes the school look bad, but it also makes the police department look incompetent."

10

Peter dribbled the ball as his team warmed up before his Special Olympics basketball game. After watching several high school basketball games, he was learning more about the concept of competitive sports. It had taken him a while to understand why so many people were into sports. Since he had not shown much of an interest until about a year ago, he was significantly behind his peers. Conversely, at the Special Olympic level, Peter was actually a step ahead of some of the other participants. Since he was high-functioning, he understood the competitive concept better and cared a little more about the outcome of the games. Basketball was a lot of fun for him, but he was often nervous when playing games. One time, he actually had a dream that he had the ball and no one between him and the basket. However, like in the dreams where you're being chased and can't run away, he dreamed that he could not run up the court to make that wide open layup.

ooooo

Joe cheered as he watched Peter and his team play. Joe had been a two-sport -standout in high school and had envisioned his only son having similar success. He certainly had to lower his expectations when watching these Special Olympic competitors. For these kids, most of the basic fundamentals were very challenging. Some of the kids were pretty competitive, but general education sporting events were totally different. Joe laughed inside as he reflected on Peter's first Special Olympics softball game at age eight. Peter was playing third base, and the base runner from the other team was currently on third base. Peter wandered over and asked his parents for a cookie.

"Peter, go back to third base!" Jennifer had exclaimed.

Peter had responded, "Oh, no need to be there, another guy came over."

Joe laughed and realized that with these events, you just couldn't take things too seriously.

As the basketball game wore on, there were indeed several comical events. One individual had the ball right underneath the basket. He proceeded to shoot it literally straight up and the ball kept coming back down into his hands. This process was repeated two or three times before the ball changed its trajectory and landed in another player's hands. Another player forgot to try to rebound the ball after a missed shot, and the ball bounced off his head instead. In one instance, when several player were trying to pick up a rapidly rolling basketball, a young girl on one of the teams picked up the ball. She then held the ball up high and yelled, "I got the ball!" Joe and numerous other spectators laughed at this. These instances weren't nearly as cute as when a small boy with Down syndrome shot the ball and then ran to his mom to give her a hug. These kids truly did have huge hearts!

ooooo

Peter actually did score four points in this game and got very excited both times and flapped his hands. Several players from his team as well as the other team patted him on the back when he made his baskets. A few moments later, Peter had a fast break to the basket and tried to be fancy like Derrick Rose from the Chicago Bulls. However, he missed the layup badly and hung his head. Joe began to yell "Peter, get your head in the…"

Just then, Jennifer put her hand on Joe, and he seemed to get the message.

"Don't worry about it, Peter. Keep playing hard," she called out.

Late in the game and with the score tied, Peter had two free throws. He was so nervous because he realized that the game was tied and several people were watching him. He had no fidget that he could squeeze to calm himself down. He ended up saying, "I love you, guys." This was a quote from Gene Hackman's character in the basketball movie *Hoosiers*. This was the best calming method available to him; however, the teenage refs, who were both guys, seemed a little baffled by that comment. Unfortunately, the ball missed pretty badly both times. Peter was so frustrated because once again, his nervousness and lack of self-confidence interfered with his being successful.

Peter's team did end up winning by a few points, so those missed free throws didn't really matter very much. What impressed Joe and Jennifer was that the players from the other team seemed so thrilled for Peter's team. They came over to Peter and his team-mates and instead of just giving the standard hand-shake, they gave them high fives and even hugs! In a world where sports can often be overly competitive and cutthroat, the innocence and spirit of Special Olympics was certainly refreshing.

ooooo

John and Kim stopped by the administration building to have another talk with Adam Cruthers and Mrs. Van Order.

"Look, I've said everything I need to say to you two, so please do your jobs and solve this crime," stammered Cruthers. "That equipment was very expensive and it was going to be a huge asset to our teachers and students!"

"Well, apparently you haven't said everything you had to say to us," teased John Scagglione. "Plus, I've missed your charming personality."

Cruthers glared and reluctantly invited the two detectives into his office.

As they entered his office, John continued, "In fact, you also failed to mention that you had two DUIs on your record, one five years ago and the other ten years ago!"

"How the heck does that implicate me in the robberies?"

"What's implicating you more than anything," said John, becoming more agitated, "is your lousy attitude with us. If you had any professionalism and would just talk to us, we wouldn't be all over you like this."

While Cruthers looked like he was about to fight, Kim stepped in and said, "The main reason we're here is because we strongly believe that someone from the district had to be behind this crime. Therefore, we're questioning all employees who have any kind of criminal background, including DUIs. It is important that we rule out all possibilities."

"Plus, that kind of behavior seems kind of irresponsible for an administrator, don't you think?" said John not willing to back far away from his bad cop role.

"Look," said Cruthers, "I am not a perfect person. I'm actually a recovering alcoholic. Maybe I'm not the most pleasant person, but I truly do care for all the kids in this district. Well, just go ahead and ask your questions. Let's get this over with."

"Okay, my first question is, where were you on the night of the robbery, and do you have an alibi?" asked Scagglione. "Tell us about your entire evening and don't leave anything out."

"Well, I should have a lawyer with me right now, but I've got lots to do and have nothing to hide. I had gone out to eat with college friends. We ate at the Olive

Garden. We left at five thirty from the district building and then came home at about seven thirty. I then watched TV with my wife until about ten thirty and then went to bed! My wife and my friend can corroborate this. Plus, I still have a receipt for the meal."

"Did you call anyone from either your house phone or your cell phone?" asked Scagglione.

"Ah, no, I don't think so."

"All right," said Scagglione. "We will need to see your phone records that night to make sure you didn't call someone suspicious, since we certainly believe that you or whoever from the district office was probably not at the robbery itself. We believe you or someone was coordinating the robbery and probably had some contact during that night by phone or email."

"Do you have a warrant for any of this information?" asked Cruthers.

"Do we need to get one?" asked Scagglione.

"No, do what you have to do. I've got nothing to hide!"

Suddenly, Kim chimed in, "What did you eat at the Olive Garden that night?"

"Geeze, what does that have to do with anything!" grumbled Cruthers. "I had linguini, garlic bread, and a tea. Do you need to know what I wore that night too?"

Ignoring that last comment, Scagglione at first was confused by Kim's question but then caught on. "Remember, there was a strong smell of garlic on the morning after the robbery." Cruthers paled. "Are you sure you weren't having dinner with your hired accomplice?"

"You can contact my friend, Adam Everest. He is a respected principal in Maple Grove, a deacon at his church, and—"

"We will certainly be contacting him as well as checking your phone messages and emails," said Kim. "Thanks for willingly providing them. However, keep in mind that although you are not yet a suspect, you are definitely a person of interest."

ooooo

After John and Kim finished their questions, Cruthers watched the two detectives move onto Mrs. Van Order. These two were trouble and would ruin his reputation as well as the district. He had many ego issues and did not like to be cornered like this. Therefore, he felt his anger for these cops and a desire to put them in their place rising. Perhaps, there was a way he could get them fired.

ooooo

John and Kim then interviewed an equally defensive Mrs. Van Order about her forced resignation from the electronics store and her former school district. They asked her the same questions about her night, and she said she had had dinner at home with her husband and teenage daughter. They had not had any garlic for dinner. She was not as willing to provide her phone records as Cruthers was, but Kim signaled to John with her eyes to not make a big deal of that right now.

"Tell us about your forced resignation from Ernie's Electronics," said Kim.

"Oh, so that's why I'm a suspect! Well, if you haven't already noticed, I do tend to be a very blunt and opinionated person. That's probably why you two are hounding me. Anyway, when I worked at Ernie's Electronics at twenty-two, my attitude certainly got the best of me and I had a fight with my manager. So they forced me to resign. Unfortunately, my mouth got me into trouble again at my first two school districts, but I am working on controlling my temper. That's why I am not absolutely screaming at you two right now."

"You are wise not to," said Scagglione. "However, you'd be more wise to provide us the information that we want including a way to contact the Ernie's Electronics store and the school districts so we can ask them their side of the story as to why you were asked to resign."

Mrs. Van Order hesitantly acquiesced, and John and Kim left with not much of a serious lead, except for the garlic clue from Mr. Cruthers.

11

John Marsch was anxious and felt that he needed another robbery job. His boss wanted to talk with him tonight. His boss, being such a clever and sneaky individual, had wanted the meeting to be in another community so as to not risk being seen by someone from Centerville. They were going to meet at the Dalton Hotel and have a meeting in the conference room. The boss had a new job for him. Although Marsch was excited, he felt that he deserved more money. Therefore, he was going to ask the boss for a raise for the next mission.

ooooo

"Throw me again, Daddy!" squealed Peter delightfully. "This is fun!" Joe bent his knees and hurled Peter in the air. Peter splashed two feet away and then swam back to his dad. "Throw me again!"

"Okay, only two more times," said Joe. Joe knew that letting Peter know how many more times he would be thrown was very important to him. It would ease the tension of having this fun activity end.

Joe marveled at how hard it had initially been for Peter to get into water. Merely touching the water as a three-year-old had caused Peter to have a meltdown. A physical therapist had had to initiate a very long process of helping Peter get used to being in a pool. It had started with him simply going into a pool area and sitting next to the water. Gradually, they worked Peter closer to the water and then had him sit with his feet in the water. Peter had gotten comfortable with that quickly and started using his finger to draw designs in the water. He seemed very fascinated with the ripples in the water.

After two more throws into the water, Joe said, "Okay, Bud, it's time to get dried off."

"Then Anne's Pizzeria?" asked Peter excitedly.

"That's right. We'll probably leave in about forty minutes."

Joe and Jennifer were excited about this opportunity to have a family night in a different town. Oftentimes, Friday nights would be spent with both of them or just Joe taking Peter to a high school sporting event. Peter seemed to be free to be himself at sporting events. When the crowds would cheer, Peter would wave his hands and go nuts. He also seemed to be fascinated by the actual games. However, this night, Joe and Jennifer felt it would be good to get out of the town since there would be much gossip and talk about the tragic week with the robbery. In fact, at the Special Olympic basketball game the day before, there had been a lot of talk including rumors in the bleachers about the robbery. Peter was okay with this change of routine since his parents had promised to take him to his favorite restaurant, Anne's Pizzeria. Even though Anne's Pizzeria did not currently serve gluten-free pizza, Joe and Jennifer took the chance of taking him there anyway since he loved it so much. Having a gluten-free diet was not necessarily a doctor's order. It was simply a general recommendation for all kids with autism. Not eating foods with gluten supposedly helped minimize the chances of kids with autism having temper tantrums or meltdowns.

"I'll have a personal pan pizza," said Peter to the server. "Please no gluten or caseins. They give me meltdowns. Also, no anchovies, they give me gas."

"Peter," admonished Jennifer.

"Oh, I'm sorry, just 'no anchovies'…I don't like them."

"I'll leave off the anchovies," said the server. "However, we don't serve gluten-free pizza."

"Oh, that's right," said Peter.

Peter was working on the social etiquette of eating at a restaurant, but sometimes tended to go into too much detail about things. *Well*, thought Joe, *it was better than when Peter was five and was on the floor screaming and crying because the menu colors had changed to red.*

After the server left, Peter said, "Anchovies, A-N-C-H-O-V-I-E-S."

Joe, Jennifer, and Peter then proceeded to have a fun family night.

After arriving back at the hotel, Peter was excited but felt that he needed a walk. Sometimes, going on walks helped him clear his mind. Usually, he would walk outside by himself, but his mom would not let him do that here at the Dalton Hotel. Therefore, his dad took him on the walk.

As Peter and Joe wandered through the halls, Peter reflected on his fun day and what he would do the next day when he got home. He would probably call Sammy, ask him to come over, and play Xbox.

Suddenly, Peter heard a familiar voice coming from inside the meeting room. He knew it real well since he never forgot voices. Then it hit him—it was the voice of someone who worked in the school district. Yet, the voice sounded very sinister and evil.

"Dad, I hear something! I know that voice!"

"What do you hear? There are a lot of voices here, Bud. We are in a hotel."

"I know who I hear talking!" said Peter as he scurried over to the wall and pressed his ear to it.

One of the benefits of Peter's autism was that he could tune out all distractions almost at will or process several things at once. Yes, there were indeed many voices at the hotel. There were kids in the pool below and other people from various rooms; however, Peter was now only focused on the voice he heard behind this wall. Yes, there was no doubt in Peter's mind whose voice he was hearing; this was the voice of the school superintendent, Mr. Steinbeck.

ooooo

"Listen, Steinbeck, I appreciate what you've been paying me," began Marsch. "But for this job, I'm going to have to double my rate. Stealing a shipment of Epson

BrightLink projectors and electromagnetic white-boards and forty major computers is a larger crime. Plus, surveillance at the district office has to be up."

"I've told you numerous times, I control the security cameras and have no trouble deleting the footage of you being in the building!" barked Steinbeck.

"Hey, if you continue cutting off info for the security cams, people are gonna get suspicious."

"First of all," said Steinbeck, "I don't pay you to think for me. You are simply paid to deliver the goods to me."

"Yeah, so you can sell those items on the black market just to make more money in addition to your massive salary. If people only knew where their tax dollars were spent."

"Listen," growled Steinbeck, "You are not my conscience! If I want to steal items from my school district, that is my business! What people don't realize about me is I'm a businessman at heart!"

"Chill out, man. I'm just messing with you. Whenever John Marsch receives an assignment, he delivers. So relax, I'll get your items. Nonetheless, stealing the Revolabs, iPads and Smart Boards was standard rate. Stealing the computers and these other items will be more risky. Therefore, my rate goes up."

"All right," conceded Steinbeck. "You'll get your money. Just keep doing things right. Even though not everyone in the community likes me, no one suspects me. Just make sure you never call me outside normal channels."

"Just one quick question," said Marsch. "If you want to make more money, why didn't you just have me take all the Smart Boards, Revolabs, and iPads? My boys and I could have handled that."

"Even though I'm ambitious and have no problem ripping off this district of snobbish taxpayers with spoiled children, I still have to be somewhat mindful of my job. In order to keep these little brats educated and performing well on ISATs, they'll need some of this equipment. I just don't think our district really needs to have every classroom in the district having a Smart Board and all the latest technological items. That's why I want a share of the profit."

ooooo

Peter trembled uncontrollably while continuing to listen despite his dad's protesting that he get away from the wall. He listened as Steinbeck and the scary other guy talked on the other side of the wall. How could this be happening! This was like being in a scary movie! Could Dr. Steinbeck really be the man who stole the items from the headquarters' building? His ears didn't lie; he had to tell his dad. The problem was, he didn't always speak clearly when he was nervous and upset. Nonetheless, he had to try.

"Peter, what's going on? What are you hearing?" insisted Joe.

"It's Steinbeck! Mr. Steinbeck's in there. He stole the school equipment."

"What?"

"It's Steinbeck! Mr. Steinbeck's in there. He stole the school equipment. I'm scared, so scared!"

"Calm down, son, let's go back to our room and talk about what you heard."

After arriving back at the room, Peter had his mom and dad's full attention.

"It's Steinbeck. Mr. Steinbeck hired a bad man. A bad man stole the supplies. He's going to steal more. It's forty computers and several electromagnetic whiteboards and Epson BrightLink projectors!"

"Whoa, Peter, slow down," said Joe.

"I can't, I'm so scared," said Peter, now in tears.

"It's okay," consoled Jennifer while hugging Peter. "Take a deep breath and tell us exactly what you heard."

"Okay," said Peter after several deep breaths. "I heard Dr. Steinbeck talking through a wall. He was saying mean things. He said, 'If I want to steal items from my school district, that is my business. What people don't realize about me is I'm a businessman at heart!'" Peter was actually able to mimic his voice almost like a professional ventriloquist. Joe and Jennifer exchanged glances and looked really scared. "The scary man said, 'Stealing the computers and these other items will be more risky. Therefore, my rate goes up.'"

"Are you sure this is what you heard? It was Mr. Steinbeck, the superintendent?" Joe said.

"Yes!" bellowed Peter. "Mr. Steinbeck also said, 'Even though not everyone in the community likes me, no one suspects me. Just make sure you never call me outside normal channels. Even though I'm ambitious and have no problem ripping off this district of snobbish taxpayers with spoiled children, I still have to be somewhat mindful of my job. In order to keep these little brats educated and performing well on ISATs, they'll need some of this equipment. I just don't think our district really needs to have every classroom in the district having a Smart Board and all the latest technological items. That's why I want a share of the profit.'"

Then Peter began to grimace. "Yuck, I smelled garlic in the room. I don't like garlic!"

"Garlic?" gasped Jennifer. "This is a hotel. There could have been garlic coming from anywhere in the building."

"No, it came from that room. The scary other guy ate a lot of garlic!"

Peter paused as he looked very overstimulated and had a distant look in his eyes. "I'm scared!" he stammered super fast. "They might hurt me."

"No one is going to hurt you," promised Jennifer. "You can stay in the room. Let's all try to relax and go to bed. Your dad and I need to decide what to do next when we go home."

12

"What are we going to do?" asked Jennifer the next morning after they arrived home.

"I think the answer to that question is obvious. We take Peter to the police. They said on the news that if anyone has any new information…"

"I don't know," stammered Jennifer. "How will Peter handle being interviewed by the police? How will they handle this news? I can't imagine they'll take him seriously because of his quirks and rate of speech."

"I'm not sure either, Honey, but we do believe Peter knows what he heard and that he's telling the truth."

"Yeah," conceded Jennifer. "Peter never lies, and when he does, he fails miserably."

Joe and Jennifer both chuckled at that truth.

"Not to mention that he always recognizes voices and can read people's voices extremely well," added Joe.

"This is just so scary, the idea that the school district that is supposed to be caring for our son is so corrupt and could be behind something like this! What will Peter reporting this to the police do? What is the next step? Will Steinbeck try to enact some kind of revenge?"

"I don't know, Hon," said Joe. "All I do know is that we have to report this to them and hope and pray that they do their jobs and follow up on this information. Also, I will not let anything happen to Peter."

When Joe called the police station, he explained that his son had overheard Supt. Steinbeck at the Dalton Hotel and wanted to tell about what he had heard.

As Joe drove Peter to the police station, his stomach was in knots. Jennifer was right; the police might not take Peter seriously. If they did, things could go either way. If Steinbeck had stolen the expensive equipment for whatever reason, that would make national headlines. Also, this would be a huge public relations disaster not just for the community, but for the whole country! This would be almost like the Catholic priest scandal. People everywhere would be outraged about a school superintendent stealing large quantities of supplies from his own district.

Joe then reflected on his own personal journey to accept Peter and be a better father. He remembered the difficulty of teaching Peter how to ride a bike at age seven. On several occasions, Joe had to remind himself not to get frustrated and make comments such as "It's not that hard, just concentrate," etc. On one particular day, Peter was whining about not being able to ride the bike—"Can't ride, can't ride, want watch *Pokemon.*"

"Bud, we can do this together. Let's try one more time, then we'll watch *Pokemon* together."

Peter echoed "one time, then Pokemon."

Joe then stood behind Peter and followed closely as Peter rode in the church parking lot and gained his balance. As Peter's momentum increased, Joe began backing off just a little.

"You're doing it, Captain!" shouted Joe. "You da man."

"You da man," repeated Peter.

"Say 'I'm the man and I can accomplish anything,'" said Joe, since Peter had so much trouble at that time understanding conversations. That day in the church parking lot was a huge milestone for Peter and for Joe.

Joe explained to Peter in the present moment, "I know you're nervous about going to talk to the police, but I'll be right there with you. We can do this together."

After Joe and his son entered the police station and talked to the receptionist, they waited for half an hour. Then a man in a dress overcoat entered and introduced himself as Detective John Scagglione. He was followed by a woman with glasses and dressed very professionally. The two detectives escorted them to Mr. Scagglione's office. Joe got the impression that Scagglione was not very comfortable talking to children. Scagglione said to Joe, "Does he want a drink?"

"I'm not sure," said Joe, feeling perturbed that once again, here was someone assuming that just because Peter had autism, he was cognitively impaired. "You'll have to ask him."

Scagglione sighed and was about to direct the question to Peter, but Peter beat him to the punch by saying "No thank you," in his quick emotionless voice.

Joe was frustrated because he felt Peter was intimidated by the detective's tone of voice. If Scagglione had been more kind and genuine, Peter may have accepted the offer.

John and Kim sat across from Peter and his dad at John's desk. John began the interview by asking Peter if he understood what the crime was that was committed.

Peter recited the facts of the case in the tone and almost exact words of a news anchor. Joe stifled a laugh, as he was amused that Peter was kind of putting Detective Scagglione in his place by showcasing his exceptional memory. Peter even quoted Scagglione's statement to the police.

Peter said, "'As a police department, we do not condone robberies of any nature, especially crimes affecting kids. We will investigate all leads and not rest until the case is solved and the criminals are brought to justice.'" The detective's facial expression showed he was truly baffled (and impressed) by Peter's reciting his statement word-for-word.

Peter concluded, "'And coming up next in weather...' Oh, sorry, I got carried away."

Joe placed a hand on Peter's shoulder and said, "That's totally okay, Bud."

ooooo

John was dumbfounded. He had heard of autism several times in his life and just always assumed that they were kids who banged their heads and screamed all the time. He had heard of, but never saw the movie *Rain Man*. This boy truly shocked him and made him rethink his views on autism. Nonetheless, he didn't want to appear overly impressed but wanted to maintain his professionalism. So he said, "Good, now that we've established that you understand the facts of the case, now tell us exactly what happened."

Peter went on to rehash what they were doing at the hotel that night, how he went on the walk with his dad and heard Dr. Steinbeck's voice through the wall, recognized that it was him and that he sounded angry.

"You were able to hear him through the wall?" asked Scagglione skeptically.

"He has a very strong sense of hearing," explained Joe. "The smallest sounds such as a paper crumbling can set him off—"

"Dad!" said Peter.

"I'm just trying to help them understand you better. I'm sorry."

"Oh, I broke a nail," Peter said sadly. The two detectives had very puzzled looks. Joe seemed puzzled at first but then said, "My son loves quoting movies. This sometimes calms him down when he gets stressed. Now, Peter, if you're going to quote an *Indiana Jones* movie, at least quote a male, not a female!"

"Okay," said Peter, rolling his eyes up as he racked his brain for a better quote, "I'll quote *Indiana Jones*." Then he said loudly, "'I hate snakes, Jacque, I hate 'em!'"

"Okay, now back to your story," said John as he did his best not to crack up. This was actually good comic relief since he himself loved the *Indiana Jones* movies.

Peter went on with his story and retold almost word-for-word what the two men said. However, Peter simply could not remember what the other man had called himself. Peter said, "Whenever...receives an assignment, whenever...receives an assignment..."

Peter then buried his hands in his face. That other guy had such a scary tone of voice. He was so afraid that this other man might come and hurt him.

"Whenever who receives an assignment?" asked an impatient Scagglione. "Was the man talking about himself in the third person? Come on, tell us."

"No, no." Peter wailed. "I want to go home, I'm so scared!"

"That's fine. Thank you very much for providing this information," said Kim. "We will definitely be looking into this. Peter, you did an excellent job telling us what happened. If you remember *anything* else, please don't tell anyone else. Call us immediately no matter how trivial it seems."

"Trivial," said Peter. "T-R-I-V-I-A-L."

When John looked at Joe quizzically, Joe said, "I'll explain later. Right now, I think Peter has had enough. I'm taking him home."

As Joe drove Peter home, he did not feel much better than he had when he brought Peter. The male detective's tone was very intimidating to Peter and made that situation much more stressful than it had to be. It was fortunate that Peter was able to explain any of the conversation at all.

"Peter, the other guy actually said his name?" asked Joe.

"Yeah, he said, 'Whenever...receives an assignment, he delivers. So relax, I'll get your items.' I can't remember the guy's name! He was scary!"

"I'm sure it will come to you, son. Don't beat your-self up. I mean, don't worry about it. You were awe-some tonight."

"Oh, no!" cried Peter. "I forgot to tell him about the garlic smell!"

"Don't worry about that detail. I'm sure that won't help them catch the guy. Try to relax, Bud. Let's relax and go get some lunch."

13

John and Kim sat in Omar Emanuel's office to discuss the latest development, which was the young autistic boy's discovery. Even though the two detectives had taped the conversation with Peter, they told the chief about the conversation using their own words.

"This kid does sound very impressive," agreed Emanuel. "However, I just don't see how much credence we can put on the word of a boy with autism," said Emanuel.

"I know, sir," began John. "I too was skeptical when the boy and his dad first walked into my office, but he is definitely a credible witness! That just blew my mind the way he recited words from the television verbatim from memory. He even sounded like the news anchor when he quoted him. Heck, he even sounded a bit like me when he quoted my words word-for-word!"

"Yes," added Kim. "He seemed like he could have been your son the way he sounded just like you. Heck, he sounded like a mini-Detective Scagglione. Anyway, I actually did read when I was in college that some kids with autism do tend to have exceptional intelligence in certain areas," reasoned Kim. "I think the word for this kind of child is *savant*. Also, he mentioned that he heard Dr. Steinbeck talking to a hired thug. That corroborates our original theory that an employee hired and provided a third party with an electronic key. Therefore, he certainly does seem to be a reliable witness."

"Anyway," said John, "he also quoted the superintendent and the other guy word-for-word. In fact, the things he reported hearing the superintendent saying were things I don't think he could have made up."

"Such as?" asked Emanuel.

"Well, the fact that Steinbeck supposedly mentioned being a businessman and not wanting to take all the Smart Boards. Steinbeck wanted to keep some so the kids would be ready for the standardized tests, but didn't think the snobbish taxpayers and their children needed to have so much technology in every classroom."

"I don't know," said Emanuel. "Some kids out there are amazingly intelligent. Kim, you yourself said this kid may be a savant, so why couldn't he have made this up?"

"My gut is telling me that he was telling the truth when he told about hearing the superintendent," said Kim.

"It sounds like you two are kind of fond of this kid," said Emanuel.

"Well, I haven't ever been much of a kid person," said John. "Most people know that about me. But man, this kid was okay. I'm not much of a sentimental guy, but this kid kind of touched my heart."

"Well, it sounds like Mr. Thick as Nails has a soft spot after all," joked Kim. "I always knew you had it in you."

"Hey, don't start expecting me to participate in the next children's assembly at school!"

"Anyway," said Emanuel, refocusing the conversation, "If this Peter Salmons is right, we're going to have to proceed with extreme caution. Arresting or simply questioning the superintendent of the school district would ruin this community. If we end up being wrong, our police department could be sued by Steinbeck for defamation of character."

"Yeah, image is everything with guys like that," muttered John.

"So what is our next step?" asked Kim. "We should at least question Andrew Steinbeck and see if he has an alibi for last Friday night? However, I can't imagine we would get any useful information let alone a confession."

"No, but maybe we can read his facial expression and reaction…" added John.

"And that would still tell us nothing!" bellowed Emanuel. "He would claim that any kind of a reaction would be because of the stress and embarrassment of being questioned by the police. We need more evidence before we move forward."

"Unfortunately, we probably can't get a search warrant based on this kid's word alone," sighed Kim.

"Yeah, that would be considered hearsay evidence," reasoned Emanuel.

"No, but surely we can possibly put surveillance on Steinbeck if we suspect we may be able to catch him in an incriminating act," said John. "If we catch him meeting this mysterious other guy, we may be able to find a license plate number. Then we could see if his accomplice has a criminal record. He may have one since he's doing the dirty work for Steinbeck."

"Yeah, such association could be enough to get a search warrant," reasoned Kim.

"All right, let's not get ahead of ourselves," interjected Emanuel. "I'll be honest with both of you. I'm leery of allocating police resources for a stakeout simply based on the word of an autistic kid. Plus, this surveillance would be on such a prominent citizen of this community!"

"Sir," pleaded John. "If this guy really is a thief, he needs to be exposed and brought down!"

"All right," conceded an exasperated Emanuel. "I'll authorize a nightly surveillance on this guy. Use an unmarked vehicle so as to not arouse suspicion."

That night, John ate at TGI Friday's with Liz and was trying to enjoy some much-needed rest and relaxation. He was actually currently involved in several cases that were currently unsolved. As Liz went on about her day, John's eyes stared ahead at the wall.

Liz, making a waving motion in front of John's face, said, "Hey, Space cadet, are you with me? Come back to earth!"

"Man, sorry. I've just got a lot on my mind. Work, you know?"

"Yeah, if we do get married, I would probably be a work widow on most nights."

"Better than being a football widow on Sundays."

"Touché," said Liz. "Seriously, you seem extra preoccupied tonight. What's up?"

"Ah, man, I interviewed a kid today. Not just any kid but one with autism."

"Interesting!" exclaimed Liz.

"Yeah, this kid actually touched my heart." John went on to explain the facts of the case. "This kid makes me want to nail this jerk Steinbeck extra badly."

After a brief pause, Liz swallowed and then began talking, "John, I have a confession to make. I feel kind of guilty myself after hearing your story. I know I've often made you feel guilty about being overly involved in various cases. Heck, that's why I left you the last time."

"That was my fault too," said John. Liz put up a hand to stop him. "Honey, as much as I love you and want to spend time with you, I don't want to hold you back on this case."

"Liz, don't! I can't lose you again."

"I'm sorry, I misled you. I'm not breaking up with you. I'm just saying do what you have to do to resolve this case and make sure you don't let me distract you. I'm with you 100 percent on this. What I'm saying is don't make time for me just out of guilt. Only call me if you truly need a break or advice."

"I do love you, Honey! Thanks for everything!"

"Well, you truly are becoming a sentimental guy!"

"All right, I hope our food gets here before I get too carried away with this soft side of me."

14

The mole inside the police station was ready to contact Andrew Steinbeck. Steinbeck was very immoral, but he was brilliant. Having a plant inside the police department was evidence of just how incredibly cunning the man was. He had recruited his plant inside the station a few years earlier. Apparently, Steinbeck was involved with a lot of white-collar crimes including laundering money and embezzling funds. He kept much of his money in off-shore accounts.

The autistic boy had somehow overheard Steinbeck and John Marsch talking! The boy and his father had entered the police station. Mr. Salmons had called saying his son had information about the District 52 crimes. After getting off work, the mole waited for the designated time and dialed Steinbeck's number. This information would be very helpful to the man.

ooooo

A few moments later, Andrew Steinbeck ended his cell phone call after talking to his plant at the police station. This was his allotted time for his cronies to call him. During this time, his wife watched her reality television shows, while Andrew would "work" in his office. After hanging up the phone, he was troubled because his perfect cover had been compromised! That darn brat, Peter Salmons with Asperger's syndrome, had somehow overheard him at the hotel! How was that possible? Even though this hearsay evidence would not be enough to obtain a search warrant, the police may begin staking out his home. Therefore, Steinbeck peeked between two blinds in his office and noticed a sedan parked about a block away from his house, and then he smiled. He would lie low, tell his people to back off and not give the cops any reason to continue pursuing him. His next planned robbery would just have to wait. Nonetheless, he would think of a way to make Peter's life miserable.

All of his life, he had planned out his schemes carefully, and things always worked out. It was his genius to hire the professional thief, John Marsch, to enter Anne's Pizzeria dressed as a server. He had planned when he would invite Mrs. Allen, her husband, and other guests to leave their table so Marsch could snatch the card from her purse. Steinbeck had observed where Allen kept her card in her purse and provided Marsch with this exact information. Heck, he had used his master manipulation skills to entice the mole from the police station to be his eyes and ears. From an early age as a young boy, he had learned to control and manipulate family and friends. He often lied to his parents and played the role of the good kid. In truth, almost everything he did, he did to get ahead in life, make more money, move up the corporate ladder, etc. He was actually addicted to risk. That is why he was willing to risk his status as district superintendent to steal the items and sell them on the black market. He was too good to let the autistic kid ruin him!

He just needed to calm his nerves and form a plan. Peter was definitely a success story in the district. The boy had started off in the low-functioning ROCKETS program, but had quickly moved into the cross-categorical classroom, and then the general education classroom receiving minimal help. The last several years, he received services only from resource teachers, social workers, counselors, and speech therapists. His current resource teacher was an idealistic, talented but young and naive first year teacher, Ms. Peggy Jones. Peter's mom was a program assistant in the ROCKETS program and was Peter's biggest advocate. She griped to him often about services for Peter, spelling bee accommodations, etc. Since in his position he didn't need to kiss up to a lowly aide, he had rarely acquiesced to her wishes. Well, now it would be fun hurting her by making Peter's life more difficult.

Steinbeck was fortunate to have two key plants or operatives within the district in administrative positions. They were both in perfect spots to cause Peter and his mother harm. His first operative, Anne Mathers, was the principal at Centerville Intermediate School. She knew Peter well, was over the staff, and would certainly be able to make administrative decisions that would not be to Peter's benefit. Steinbeck did know that Peter had a history of having meltdowns.

Perhaps, Mathers could stymie Peter's progress in that area and cause him to be placed in the county's alternative behavior disorder program.

His other operative was Jim Shurna, the coordinator of the ROCKETS program. It was possible that Jim could somehow find a reason to fire Jennifer as an aide! That would show her that she and her family should not mess with him. Although Jennifer would certainly call bloody murder, if Steinbeck and his friends were careful, there would be no evidence against them.

Now, Andrew was ecstatic! Before Peter and Jennifer took him down, he would take them down. These two administrators were his recruits and old friends. They had also risen to high positions in the school district as he had. Andrew had had enough clout to make sure that they got hired. As far as Andrew knew, most of the rest of the faculty in the district were moral, ethical, and professional people. For him, Mathers and Shurna, these attributes were mostly a ruse. He grabbed his cell phone to make the necessary calls. He would certainly call Marsch and his Iraq war veteran buddies to tell them to lie low for a while.

ooooo

Anne Mathers got to work immediately and began formulating an idea. This would be tricky, because she legally could not change Peter's IEP and take away his services without a team meeting and parent permission. However, perhaps she could make some executive decisions to hurt Peter's routine. She knew that the real key to causing Peter to fail was cutting off his support network. Peter was susceptible to angry outbursts if he was pushed far enough, therefore, she needed to manipulate his schedule enough to get him away from his two best friends, Betsy and Sammy. They were his calming influence in the school setting. The first step would be to tweak Peter's schedule so he would have his lunch changed, and he would be placed in a lunch not only away from Betsy and Sammy, but in a lunch with Frank O'Day. Yes, Frank could have a field day, and it would be open season on Peter!

Mathers felt a slight bit of guilt for intentionally putting a kid with a disability in harm's way. However, she reasoned that Frank probably would not really hurt Peter. Frank was a bully, often doing little things to Peter like shoving or lightly punching him in order to get a reaction out of him. These reactions were key to helping rid the district of Peter. It wasn't like Frank would completely maim Peter. In addition to setting up Frank to pick on Peter, she would also schedule several staff meetings involving the speech therapist and social worker who would disrupt Peter's scheduled times. Also, she would implement several power bell schedules to cause shorter class periods. This would make it harder for the teachers to teach in a manner that would benefit Peter. Lessons would be hurried, accommodations would be minimal, and this would frustrate Peter.

Finally, Mathers would look to use her powers to remove Peter's accommodations that were not specified in his IEP. All this stress would cause Peter to snap several times, and then the district may be able to ship him off to the alternative program! Ultimately, Mathers figured having Peter shipped off to the alternative school would benefit the other students. American society was so obsessed with equality and fairness and often went overboard with it. This liberal agenda was so strong in the school system that many educators believed in full inclusion of kids with disabilities. Although Peter was a nice kid, having him in an alternative school would certainly benefit him and everyone else.

15

During the next couple of weeks, Mather's plan was implemented. When Peter was not allowed to sit in front of his math class, he became very agitated. Math was already more difficult of a subject than his other classes. Mr. Appleton explained to Peter that he wanted to challenge him to not have to depend on sitting in front of the class.

This accommodation was initiated so Peter could eliminate distractions, but it was not specified in his IEP. Peter could tell that Mr. Appleton did not really believe in what he was doing, but he enforced this new rule anyway. Also, he was not allowed to have the red timer that helped him know how much longer a test would be. He still received extended time on tests, which *was* specified on his IEP. However, not having the timer made Peter very anxious. In fact, during a social studies test, he screamed "No fair, I need more time!" when the teacher said it was time for the kids to go back to their homeroom class. Peter then threw his pencil and it hit a girl in the back. Even though there was minimal pain, Peter had to sit in the principal's office. That day in the lunch room, Frank approached Peter, who was eating alone.

"Oh, where is your girlfriend and boyfriend?" teased Frank. "Oh, are they not around to wipe your nose?" Frank quickly snatched one of Peter's pretzels. Peter, who was already extremely anxious about his bad test experience, his schedule change, and having missed his social work session, snapped.

"Give that back! Get away from me."

"Oh, don't throw a pencil at me," whined Frank mockingly. Instead, Peter threw his chocolate milk at Frank, and some of it hit other students. Peter was in big trouble for that incident. He was forced to clean the mess and got to spend more time with Principal Mathers.

For the next several days, things continued in this pattern for Peter. Since Mathers then began enforcing the power bell schedules, classes did indeed become more hectic and less predictable, and Peter became more stressed. Another move by Mathers was removing the covered lights in the classrooms. The flickering lights overstimulated and greatly increased Peter's stress level. Mathers had explained to the teachers that covering the lights was an added expense to a district in financial ruin after the robberies. She also expressed that having Peter exposed to the lights as they were would better prepare him for the real world. Frank and his punk friends continued to antagonize Peter in the lunch room and hallway. The problem was Frank and his buddies were sneaky enough to provoke Peter when other staff members' heads were turned. When Frank was engaged in shoving Peter in the head or lightly punching him, Peter would react by whining, throwing food, and two-handed slapping or kicking. The issue was that these self-defense techniques were often uncoordinated and clumsy. Unfortunately, the staff always caught Peter's reaction instead of Frank instigating the fights.

Jennifer and Joe were alarmed at this chain of events and naturally called the school to find out what was going on. Mathers articulated very clearly her untruthful explanation for the need for removing the accommodations, having the power bell schedules, and the lunch change. Even though they had no real reason to believe Principal Mathers was involved in the crimes with Andrew Steinbeck, they figured there must have been a connection. This was confusing because Steinbeck had no way of knowing that Peter had snitched on him, unless the police had leaked that information. It was just too coincidental to have all this happening to Peter immediately after the hotel incident. Jennifer demanded an emergency meeting with the school.

ooooo

At the emergency meeting, Mathers began with her typical pleasant greeting. She then continued by explaining about the many documented incidents of Peter's actions for the last several weeks. Jennifer did concede that Peter's behavior had escalated at home, but she was still ticked off by all the changes in Peter's routine. Mathers once again justified her actions, but then went on to explain what she and Assistant Superintendent Adam Cruthers felt needed to be done.

She explained, "We have several students at this school whose education is being disrupted because of Peter's outbursts and meltdowns. We do truly want what's best for Peter, but in light of this alarming chain of events, we feel that it would currently be appropriate for Peter to be either home-schooled or placed at the alternative school."

"You people can't be serious!" stammered Joe. "This is absolute crap and all of you know it!"

"We know you're upset," explained Adam Cruthers, "but I also feel that these documented incidents justify a change in Peter's education setting. He has certainly regressed—"

"Not going to happen!" remarked Jennifer. "Peter is not going to go to an alternative school. How dare you tell us to either go along with your wishes, or home-school Peter! Peter is a wonderful kid with a great heart. He deserves the same education as all the other kids do. We know our rights and will contact a lawyer if you continue this."

"Mr. and Mrs. Salmons," said Mathers soothingly, "Peter *is* a wonderful kid and we've enjoyed having him here at Centerville Intermediate School. This course of action is not something we are taking lightly. We are doing what is in the best interest of the kids."

"Don't start again with talking about how you people are looking out for the best interests of the kids!" Jennifer practically shouted. "You people in this district just look out for your own interests. In fact, I'm so angry right now that I'm considering telling everyone, including the media, what I think. I think you people are in a conspiracy with Andrew Steinbeck to hurt Peter!"

Everyone at the table gasped, including Joe, who gave his wife a look that warned her not to say anything else.

A stunned Peggy Jones, who had kept her mouth shut the entire meeting, asked, "Why would there be a conspiracy against Peter?"

Jennifer, on the verge of tears now, kept her mouth shut knowing that she may have inadvertently caused more harm to Peter.

Joe explained calmly, "We're both just upset. We don't agree with what the school district is doing and we have stress in our personal lives." Joe was referring to the whole investigation involving Steinbeck. "Please just hold off on placing Peter in the alternative program."

"I'll tell you what," said a composed Jennifer. "I'll keep Peter home for a week to see if he calms down. You can send him all his schoolwork, and I'll even deliver it to you each day. This will give everyone time to cool down, and then we'll decide what do to."

Everyone agreed that this was the best course of action.

ooooo

As Peggy Jones drove home, tears began pouring down her face. What was that meeting all about? She was so confused. As Peter's resource teacher, she had been baffled by all the mysterious changes implemented by Mrs. Mathers. She, the social worker, speech therapist, and several other staff truly disagreed with these actions. They had all tried desperately to help Peter cope with these weird changes, including the many cancelled therapy sessions. Peggy absolutely disagreed with changing Peter's placement so quickly, especially after his behavior had only escalated in such a short time.

What if Peter's parents were right? Could there be some conspiracy involving Steinbeck and the administration setting up Peter to fail? Why did Peter's mom feel that way? Had something happened? If there was something going on, could she really take a stand against the district? She had done most of her education observation hours and her student teaching here in District 52. Cruthers, Steinbeck, and Mathers had all been mentors to her, supported her, and ultimately hired her to teach. Teaching had been her goal since she had participated in a reading buddies program with kids with disabilities back in middle school. How can a first year, non-tenured teacher fight the administration? That would truly be like biting the hand that feeds you. However, could she live with herself if she went along with sabotaging the life of a boy with Asperger's? Peggy sighed. She would try to relax tonight and not think about school. She and her boyfriend, Doug, were going to a performance of *Joseph and the Amazing Technicolor Dreamcoat* tomorrow night. He had bought the tickets as an anniversary present. Nonetheless, how could she conceal her stress? Doug always seemed to see right through her and would definitely know something was up. The stress of this situation was almost too much to handle. College simply had not prepared her for this kind of predicament!

ooooo

As Adam Cruthers settled in for the night, he felt that something was indeed off. Although he had been concerned about Peter's escalating behavior and agreed with Mrs. Mathers that changing his placement might be best, this whole situation was bothering him. Andrew Steinbeck had been acting strangely the past month. Jennifer's words about a conspiracy certainly bothered him. Although Cruthers did have a blunt personality, he truly cared about the kids and the staff who worked under him. It bothered him that Steinbeck never seemed to take Peter's mom or other program assistants seriously. These program assistants were the employees who did the unpleasant jobs like changing dirty diapers and taking the brunt of kids' tempers, either by being hit or spit on. They truly worked in the trenches. When Jennifer had mentioned a conspiracy, that had triggered something in his memory. He just couldn't figure out what. Cruthers sat in his hot tub and tried to ponder what he could do to act on his suspicions.

ooooo

That night, Peter sensed from the way his mom and dad talked that they were upset. He grabbed his sheet and squeezed it tightly. This was his ultimate stress relief. Playing under the sheets entailed him sitting under it, squeezing it, and imagining making movies. With all his troubles at school, he found himself playing under the sheets more often. Although he knew this was not really socially appropriate or at least a typical behavior, it was *his* way of dealing with the world. Ms. Jones had often worked with him these first few months of school on finding replacement behaviors. These are behaviors that are socially more appropriate that replace the inappropriate behaviors. One such example was when he felt that he needed to scream in class. His replacement behavior was holding up a color-coded piece of paper to signal that he needed a sensory break. However, he just could not find a replacement behavior for playing under the sheets; therefore, playing under the sheets would remain his favorite activity.

16

On Friday afternoon, Jennifer proceeded with caution as she walked into the office of Jim Shurna. Although she had a great deal of respect for the ROCKETS program coordinator, she often disagreed with his management style. Several times, she also did not see eye-to-eye with the young teachers she often worked under. Jennifer thought these young teachers sometimes acted like they knew everything coming out of college. This was annoying because Jennifer had a child with autism and she felt that after three years in the program, she had some expertise!

She took a seat as Mr. Shurna began, "I understand your last evaluation was not the best. Please first of all share about your perceptions on it."

"Well," began Jennifer, already not liking the start of this meeting, "I feel much of Ms. Anderson's accusations are off-base. It seemed as if several of her remarks were in vague reference to situations where she spun things around to make me the bad guy. I also can't fathom why me worrying about safety is a bad thing. Anyway, I'm trying to have a good attitude about the evaluation. I will try to take it positively and use it to improve myself as an aide."

"Well, this is indeed very hard. However, I do have deep concerns about your having ongoing difficulty getting along with your supervising teachers."

"Excuse me, have I ever *not* done something a teacher has told me to do?" said Jennifer as her blood pressure was getting higher.

"Still, it seems when you do question your teachers, your tone is threatening, as it is now. It is very important for the kids that all the staff get along and that there is a united front in the classroom. Therefore, man, this is hard! Therefore, the administration and I have decided that it would be in your best interest, and the kids' as well, if you step down."

Jennifer's jaw dropped; she was too angry to speak. Finally, she managed to force herself to talk. "You mean it's in *your* best interest, and probably Andrew Steinbeck's too! I bet he's behind this, isn't he?"

"Jennifer, don't make this harder than it already is. I would like you to write a letter of resignation. I know you don't believe me now, but I sincerely wish you the best of luck."

"I'm not writing anything."

"Please, Jennifer, if you don't, we have no choice but to move forward and terminate your employment."

Jennifer stormed out of the office and did not look back.

ooooo

That night, Peter's friends—Betsy, Sammy, and a new friend in their group, Freddy Gorski—came over to hang out and play Xbox. The kids were very curious as to why Peter was going to have a week of vacation. Although Jennifer and Joe didn't plan on doing this, they shared with them about Peter's school troubles. All three of them knew things were going badly for Peter. Jennifer was especially shaken because of Peter's situation and her shocking news. Joe had earlier suggested that they call a lawyer to fight the cooperative. The only problem was there was no union for aides in the cooperative, and their contracts gave the administration the right to terminate an aide's employment at any time with valid cause. Even though Jennifer did not feel they had probable cause, the cooperative felt otherwise and used her past evaluations as justification for this action.

"I don't want to go back to school," whined Peter. "No more Frank, no more Frank, school makes me unhappy."

"Peter, you have to go back sometime. We just have to figure out what to do," said Joe.

"Why did they switch Peter's lunch and gym?" asked Betsy. "That was just wrong!"

"I hate to say it, but I think the reason they did it was to get Peter away from you and Sammy so you couldn't support him anymore," said Jennifer. "If that is the case, then I think we should absolutely not make Peter go back to an environment where the school is trying to hurt him! I really think we need to call a lawyer."

"Why would the school do something like this?" asked Freddy, who seemed paranoid about the idea of the school being involved in such a conspiracy.

"Yeah, I've been wondering the same thing," said Sammy. "Everything that's been happening has seemed very fishy."

Jennifer and Joe exchanged glances, both not sure just how much information they should give to these ten- and eleven-year-olds. After being given an approving nod from his wife, Joe prayed silently that he was doing the right thing and then told part of the story.

"Peter heard a school official having a conversation that he wasn't supposed to hear. Peter now knows who stole the school equipment."

"So it was somebody who worked at the school?" Sammy asked.

"Yes, it was Mr. Steinbeck," blurted Peter, who then began to recite exactly what he heard.

"Peter," interrupted Jennifer, "you weren't supposed to tell anyone."

"Sorry, it was an accident," said Peter as he flapped his hands.

"This is scary!" exclaimed Betsy.

"So anyway," continued Joe, "we don't know for sure, but we think Dr. Steinbeck may be trying to get back at Peter for reporting what he heard to the cops."

"Why don't the cops just arrest Mr. Steinbeck?" asked Freddy, who knew nothing about the justice system.

"It's not that simple," explained Joe. "In order for the cops to arrest him, they need to catch Mr. Steinbeck doing something wrong or they have to find evidence that would prove he stole the equipment or is doing something illegal."

"They also have to get a search and an arrest warrant, right?" asked Sammy.

"That's basically how it works, right," said Joe.

"This is just maddening," exclaimed Jennifer, now in tears. "Before, I wasn't so sure, but now I am positive that Steinbeck is behind this, and so is Mrs. Mathers. I'm sure Mr. Shurna from the ROCKETS program is in on this too and that's why I lost my job."

"You lost your job?" remarked Betsy.

"What's the ROCKETS program?" asked Freddy.

Peter then began to recite what ROCKETS stood for, but Jennifer cut him off by saying, "We'll explain later what the ROCKETS program is. Right now, I just don't see how we can even think of letting Peter return to that school. On Monday morning, I want to begin the process of removing Peter from the school and begin homeschooling him."

"Honey, I understand where you're coming from," explained Joe. "I'm scared too for Peter, but a part of me says we can't just let the school district win—"

"How can you say that when your own son, our baby, is going to school in an environment where he is being bullied, harassed, and the principal and superintendent are behind it!" stammered Jennifer, now completely hysterical.

"Oh my goodness," wailed Peter, now crying himself. "I won't go back to school. Please help! Please help!"

Peter then ran off because he couldn't stand seeing his mom cry, and the stress of the situation was way too much for him. The three other kids sat frozen, watching the two parents have this argument. Jennifer continued to cry and Joe himself buried his hands in his face.

"We're sorry, kids," said Jennifer.

"That's okay," said Betsy. She paused and then continued, "Mr. and Mrs. Salmons, I know I'm just a kid, but I think I have an idea."

ooooo

Allan Huisenga put his foot on the break pedal to avoid being seen by John Scagglione and Kim Madigan. It had been a long time since he had tailed anyone. His timing was slightly off, but he instinctively knew how to stay far enough behind but still close enough to keep up with a target. He used to follow suspects of various crimes. This situation was completely different since he was following two other cops while off duty. He knew this could certainly cost him his career, but after all these years on the force, he really didn't care. The police profession was as corrupt and political as any institution. He believed in his heart that he deserved to be chief and was certainly bitter about being passed over for the job. Kim pulled the sedan over to the curb, and the two remained parked for a long period of time. It was obvious that they were staking out Andrew Steinbeck's home. They were probably not going to catch him doing anything incriminating since Steinbeck was a smart man. Allan sipped his coffee as he waited patiently and kept an eye on the two cops. He would watch them for a while before returning home and retiring for the night.

ooooo

Betsy now had the attention of all four of them. She felt nervous knowing that she was only in fifth grade! Who was she to plan a strategy of standing up to the principal and superintendent of her school? She then remembered the fear in Peter's eyes and this reinvigorated her resolve. She braced herself, took a deep breath, and then shared her thoughts. "Peter showed me some of those special stories that his social worker and teacher wrote for him. What are they called?"

After a slight pause, Jennifer said, "Oh, they're called social stories."

"Well, if Mrs. Mathers and Mr. Steinbeck *want* Frank to be picking on Peter, then Peter needs to stand up to Frank in the cafeteria. I've seen several times how Frank tries to upset Peter. First of all, Freddy, aren't you in Peter's lunch?"

"Yeah, I've seen Frank pick on him several times, I just never know what to do."

"Okay, my idea is that maybe we can write a social story about how Peter can stand up to a bully, specifically Frank."

"I guess that's an idea," said Joe.

"I'll have to think about this," said Jennifer. "I'm still keeping him home for at least a week."

"Actually," said Sammy, "Keeping Peter home is a great idea! I can teach Peter martial arts, and Peter can train while he stays home. I'll practice with him after school, and when he goes back to school, he'll be ready to kick butt."

"I don't want Peter fighting. I don't like that idea," exclaimed Jennifer. "Plus, Peter keeps getting caught for lashing out at Frank."

"I'm sorry," said Sammy. "I forgot what I've been taught. Martial arts is for self-defense only. I'll only teach Peter how to block punches and kicks. Martial arts will help Peter stay calm and confident when Frank tries to pick on him."

"This is perfect," said Betsy. "Mrs. Salmons, you know how to write social stories, right?"

"I've been trained but don't have much experience writing them. I'm only an aide. The teachers write the social stories and they never have asked me to help."

Betsy looked disappointed, and Jennifer continued, "However, with the training I have received at various in-services, I think I can successfully put one together."

"Great. You can write the story, and I'll help tell you what cool things a fifth grader can say to stand up to a bully. While I help you with that, Sammy will train Peter to stand up for himself."

"What can I do to help?" asked Freddy.

"Since you are in Peter's lunch, you can help him if he needs extra help."

"This is weird," said Freddy. "It's kind of like we are an army secret mission group preparing for a dangerous mission! We are a kid squadron!"

"Yeah, we are kind of like an undercover group," agreed Joe. "Only, this mission involves putting my son in harm's way, and I'm a little uncomfortable with this. However, I guess Peter needs to learn to stand up for himself."

"Joe," said Jennifer, "I think you should probably call Detective Scagglione and let him know what the school is doing and what our plan of action is."

ooooo

After several weeks of unproductive surveillance on Steinbeck and pursuing other dead-end leads, Kim was becoming frustrated. Steinbeck was living a normal life and following a normal routine. He was probably lying low, but Kim and John could not figure out how that was possible. The police department hadn't gone public about the latest lead on the theft. As they sat watching Steinbeck's house on a rainy Friday night, John received a phone call.

"Scagglione," answered John.

John said a lot of "uh huhs" and "ohs." Then he seemed to be getting distressed. Finally, he blurted out, "You told a bunch of kids! This could ruin the whole investigation!"

After he listened for a few more minutes, he calmed down but still admonished Mr. Salmons to "please consult me before informing anyone else about the investigation!"

After an exasperated John hung up, he told Kim about the district apparently knowing about Peter being an eyewitness, and that the powers that be in the district were apparently trying to cause Peter to have to leave the school for the alternative program. He then informed Kim about the Salmons telling Peter's young friends about what Peter heard and the strange renegade mission they were on to help Peter stand up to Frank, the school bully.

"Joe Salmons told me that these kids are all good kids and best friends of Peter, and that they're totally trustworthy, but, man, this case is really starting to worry me!"

"Yeah, especially now that it's involving innocent kids," agreed Kim. "I just hope we can catch Steinbeck doing something incriminating before things get more out of hand."

As they continued their stakeout, Kim became more anxious. The possibility that the school apparently knew about Peter talking to the police aroused another more scary possibility. If Steinbeck knew that Peter was onto him and was retaliating to make his life miserable, there was a horrible possibility that there was a mole inside the police station. Kim did not want to dwell on this too much because that would be horrible. Who could she trust then? Should she tell John about her thought? That would not be wise in case *he* was the mole. Who else at the station knew about what was going on. Christine Jensen was the receptionist and surely took the call from Peter's dad. Could she have told someone else? Chief Emanuel was the only one other than John or Kim who knew all the facts of the case. The other possibility was Allan Huisenga, who was very bitter about being passed over for the position of being chief. In fact, if Steinbeck was so corrupt, there was a chance this conspiracy went as far as to the mayor's office! Who could be trusted? This was indeed a headache that Kim did not want to think about too deeply.

17

As Peggy and Doug drove home from the musical, Doug was in his usual mode of critiquing the performance. That had always been his nature; he was a natural critical thinker. He had enjoyed staying up late in college and debating politics, philosophy, religion, and many other topics deep into the night. However, tonight Peggy was not herself. She usually liked to debate with him when he acted this way. This was one of the reasons they were a good couple. She could go head-to-head with him in a debate.

"Honey, please tell me what's wrong and don't give me that 'I'm fine' crap."

Peggy sighed and then said, "Dang, you always see right through me! Why can't you be dense and naive like so many other guys?"

"Hon, I keep telling you, when God made me, he broke the mold."

Peggy playfully punched Doug and then told her story about what was going on at the school. She explained that she had a strong hunch about the connection between the school robberies and Peter's poor fortune. She figured that maybe Peter knew something about what happened and the district was trying to put him in his place.

"I mean, they have to be trying to hurt him. All these changes in his program are just too coinciden- tal, and the reasons they gave me for taking away the accommodations initially made sense, but now they seem bogus. Plus, his mom just lost her job as an aide at the ROCKETS program."

"ROCKETS?"

"It's the program serviced by the county cooperative that takes care of students with more severe autism. I actually observed some of those classrooms during my student teaching observation hours."

"Man, I've always loved conspiracy theories and critiquing the school system," said Doug. "But this is strange! I never thought a major conspiracy and cor- ruption in the school system would directly affect someone I love. This is ridiculous! You are so passionate about your work and helping those kids."

"I know, but I'm so confused about what to do now. If they are trying to hurt Peter, I can't live with myself if I do nothing. Yet, I'm only a first year teacher."

"Here's what I think, Hon. Don't make any drastic moves or say anything right away. Lie low and kind of play detective for a while. If you see anything that gives evidence to your theory or find a way you can help Peter when he comes back to school, then take action."

ooooo

Sammy took a deep breath as he poised himself to begin training Peter to stand up for himself against Frank. He knew that Betsy and Mrs. Salmons had been working on and reading that social story thing to help Peter, which was supposedly going to get him ready and help him stay calm when Frank tried to pick on him. Frank always got Peter rattled by making sneaky comments and occasionally pushing or punching him. However, Frank knew not to mess with Sammy since he was a brown belt in karate.

Sammy had known Peter since first grade. In the earlier grades, kids sometimes made initiatives to say hi to Peter and encourage him to play with them. There had even been an autism expert, whom Sammy thought he remembered being called an itinerant, who had spoken to the entire first grade class about Peter and autism. Peter had seemed weird to Sammy at that time because Peter became so agitated when the smallest thing such as a removed poster was taken down from the wall. Peter's one-on-one aide at the time would have to take him out of the classroom if he began screaming and yelling. The people who worked with him always called this a meltdown. Peter also seemed strange because he had been completely obsessed with dinosaurs and trains. Despite his quirks, Betsy had always been kind to Peter, even in first grade. Peter had not attended kindergarten with the regular kids since he was still in the ROCKETS program.

In fourth grade, kids started to tease him more. There had been a day early in the year when some kids told Peter he couldn't play baseball with them at recess.

Sammy, who had been a little nervous about being made fun at, decided to be brave and said, "Let's give him a chance. Let him play." The other kids eyed Sammy with annoyed glances, but decided to let him play.

Several kids during the game had made fun of Peter's form of throwing the baseball. When they continually mimicked his technique and said he threw like a girl, Sammy had had enough. In Sunday School, Sammy had learned about loving your neighbor and being nice to people who were not like you. Sammy then told the other kids to leave Peter alone, and since Sammy was an athletic kid, he had some clout, and other kids respected him. They had then backed off of Peter, but Sammy's popularity did sink a little the next year and a half. Throughout the rest of that year and during the summer between fourth and fifth grade, Sammy had tried without much success teaching Peter how to throw a baseball without looking so awkward. That skill just did not come naturally for Peter. Now, Sammy had the much tougher task of teaching Peter to fight back against a major bully.

"Okay, Peter, when Frank tries to punch or push you, you've got to be able to block them."

"Oh, like in *The Karate Kid*—wax on, wax off," said Peter, mimicking Ralph Machio's words and movements from the movie.

"Yeah, exactly like that, dude," laughed Sammy. "However, when Frank comes at you, the first thing you want to do is stand sideways to him. That will make it harder for him to hit you." Sammy then demonstrated the stance.

"Stand sideways, like *Sideways Stories from Wayside School*," gloated Peter, who seemed proud of himself for making this connection.

"Peter, dude, focus," said Sammy, trying to maintain his patience. Nonetheless, it was kind of cool how Peter's mind worked making so many goofy connections.

"Sorry," said Peter. "I need to focus like Daniel-san. 'Daniel-san, you must focus.'" This was another quote from *The Karate Kid*.

"Oh, I'm sorry," said Peter who looked worried that he might have upset Sammy.

"That's okay."

Sammy went on to work with Peter on how to block punches and kicks if necessary. He emphasized to Peter that he needed to block with the soft part of his forearm in order to keep himself from getting hurt. Unfortunately, when Sammy tried to have Peter practice blocking a pretend punch, Peter's block missed Sammy's punch. Instead, the block landed square in Sammy's eye.

"Oh, I'm so sorry! Don't be mad," begged Peter.

"No, that's fine," said Sammy, who had to blink away a watering eye. "I guess that's one way to fight back. Just land a block into Frank's face."

Peter chuckled but didn't appear to get the joke.

The two of them continued to practice for the next few days. When Peter began getting the concept, Sammy worked him a little harder in order to prepare him for the real thing against Frank. Freddy also attended some of the sessions. He also wanted to learn some self-defense techniques in case he needed to help defend Peter. In fact, Sammy actually had Freddy and Peter spar with boxing gloves. Peter at first said, "Oh, yuck, yuck, red, I don't like red."

"It's okay," said Sammy. "Deal with it." Sammy thought that if Peter overcame his fear of red, he would have an easier time standing up to Frank. As Peter and Freddy began sparring, Peter at first looked like he was bouncing in a moonwalk. He had the correct stance, but he just looked so awkward. Sammy prayed for patience.

When Freddy socked Peter in the face, Peter ran, buried his hands, and started yelling, "Stop, stop, leave me alone!"

"Peter," coached Sammy. "Don't get upset. That's what Frank wants. Come back over and block Freddy's punch."

As Peter slowly returned, Freddy began to throw another jab, but Peter blocked it nicely. "All right, hero, have enough," said Peter.

A puzzled Freddy looked at Sammy, who explained, "*The Karate Kid*, Peter's Mr. Movie Man. He likes saying lines from movies."

As the two boys continued sparring, Peter let out a loud fart. Freddy darted for cover and hid behind the couch. Sammy waived his hand in front of his face and said, "Whew, that was nasty, man!"

"Sorry," said Peter. "It was an accident."

"It's all good, Peter. Well, that will definitely make Frank run away."

After a few more minutes, Freddy came out of his hiding place and asked, "Is it safe now?" After several more sessions, Peter was actually becoming very comfortable with blocking.

∞∞∞

The night before Peter's return to school, Joe and Jennifer discussed how they felt about sending Peter back. "I just can't believe we're letting him go back to the school!" stammered Jennifer. "This whole thing with the social story, him learning martial arts, seems like a social experiment. We can't do this! Peter has to stay home until we figure out for sure what's going on."

"I know, Honey, I've been fighting with myself over this same thing. Again, I just think we have to let Peter go to school. If we have him always run away from his problems, that will hurt him in the long run."

"Yes, but don't you think this problem is kind of extreme. For goodness' sake, the school is intentionally trying to hurt him!"

"Honey, don't get mad. We can't be absolutely 100 percent certain that they are behind this…"

"Please don't go there, I just know they're behind this…"

"Well, why don't we call the school tomorrow, tell them about our reservations and that if Peter has trouble, we will take them to court. That will hopefully convince them to at least try to protect Peter. Also, why don't I give Peter my cell phone to use in case things do get out of hand tomorrow. If Frank's completely harassing him, Peter can call you and you can pick him up."

18

After hearing more about the Kid Squadron Plan, John shook his head. He couldn't really believe the parents were letting the kids go through with this plan of action while calling themselves Kid Squadron. This wasn't a game! Mr. Salmons had explained that using the title "Kid Squadron" was just to lighten the mood of the situation. John had a good mind to go to the school and follow Peter around all day to keep him safe. However, a cop following a fifth grader around all day would certainly look bizarre. Since he wasn't sure what to do, he called Liz.

"Absolutely do not go to the school," she admonished him. "I agree this is nerve-racking and risky, but this kid probably does need to stand up for himself. If he succeeds at this, then the school has failed. If you follow him around, the school will probably win. The district may even use the fact that you're following him around as justification for removing him from the school."

"Liz, you have amazing insight."

"Just remember that when we begin planning our wedding!"

ooooo

Peter was nervous as he, Freddy, Sammy, and Betsy all walked to school together. They were all supporting him as were his parents. Peter knew he had to be a big boy today and be very calm and cool if Frank tried to pick on him. His mom had read with him the social story countless times that she and Betsy had written for him. The story had said this:

> If Frank says mean things to me, it is okay. Frank feels bad about himself, and that is why he picks on me. When he picks on me, I will try to stay calm and not yell and throw food at him. Instead of being scared and angry, I can stand up to Frank by teasing him back. I am very smart and can use my brain to outwit him. One thing I can say is that "I hope teasing me makes you feel good. However, your stupid ways will not bother me. Get a life." If Frank calls me a mean name, I can say, "Eh, takes one to know one." If he tries to touch me, I will not get mad. I will calmly block his pushes and punches and say, "You're not as tough as you thought."

Peter also felt comforted that he had his dad's cell phone in case he needed to call his mom. Cell phones were not allowed in school, and Peter did feel uneasy about breaking a school rule. Nonetheless, his parents assured him, as they had several times, that there were times in life when breaking or bending the rules was necessary.

ooooo

Although Freddy was fairly new to Peter's friendship group, he cared for his new friend. He hoped he would have the courage to do his job of standing up for Peter if necessary in the cafeteria. Part of the reason he had not stood up for Peter before was because he was kind of afraid of Frank. In truth, Frank had occasionally picked on him before. If Freddy tried to stand up for Peter, there was no doubt in his mind that Frank would then come after him. Therefore, it was always easier for Freddy to simply avoid Frank and do nothing when he picked on other kids.

As they walked to school, Betsy reassured both of them. "Peter, you can do this. You are very smart, and Frank is really a coward. Freddy, please be ready just in case Peter needs help."

ooooo

Adam Cruthers stepped out of the administration building and finally worked up the courage to do what he felt he needed to do. After Jennifer's firing as a para-professional, things started to come together for him. First, there had been the school robberies. Shortly after that, Steinbeck had begun acting strangely. Then Anne Mathers had instituted the changes in Centerville Intermediate School. This led to Peter having severe meltdowns, and Mathers had convinced him to suggest to Peter's parents to have him placed in the alternative school. Peter's mom had accused them of being involved in a conspiracy, and the day after that, she had been fired as a program assistant.

In fact, Jennifer had been one of the best program assistants in the ROCKETS program in Cruther's opinion. He did not agree with the young teachers who had had issues with her. Since Jennifer had a child with a disability and was older than much of the other staff, she was naturally opinionated and very caring for the children.

Anyway, Adam finally remembered what it was that had happened several years earlier that tied into what was presently going on. When the district had hired Anne Mathers and Jim Shurna to be the principal and the ROCKETS coordinator respectively, neither Adam nor several members of the school board had wanted to hire them. Steinbeck had used his clout and political influence to get them hired. Was it possible they had been friends before? After all, if there was a conspiracy going on, they were in key positions to help him hurt Peter and his mom. He called detectives John Scagglione and Kim Madigan, who had antagonized him and upset him initially, and explained his theory.

ooooo

Peter sat at his table eating his lunch, his heart pounding very fast. He took several deep breaths and felt even better after seeing Freddy give him a thumbs-up. As

Peter began eating his lunch, Frank approached him. However, instead of getting more nervous, a surprising calm actually took hold of Peter. It was as if the waiting for this moment was the most agonizing. Having it finally be here in some ways was a relief. "Hey, Pete, we missed you last week. Where were you at? You too scared to come to school?"

Peter actually remembered the part of the social story that read: "I am very smart and can use my brain to outwit him." He then thought to himself, *this is improper grammar! I cannot let this happen!*

"Hey, Frank," began Peter in his typical voice. Changing to a more normal tone, he continued, "That is improper grammar. I'm so disappointed. Never end a sentence with a preposition! What you should have said…was 'Where were you? *Were* you too scared to come to school?'"

Frank looked at his two punk friends, smirked at them, and recovered from his momentary confusion at Peter's new reaction. "You are such a loser and a nerd," sneered Frank.

"Eh, takes one to know one,?" chided Peter after a brief pause.

"Ha-ha-ha-ha," jeered Frank, slapping his own chest in mockery of kids with cognitive impairment.

"You are part of the rebel alliance and a traitor…" *No, I do not want to quote Star Wars right now!* " I hope teasing me makes you feel good! However, your stupid ways will not bother me. You are the one with the problem. Get a life!"

By now, several other kids in the cafeteria were quietly watching this exchange.

"Shut your mouth, you loser," growled Frank. "I'm going to beat you up!"

"Wow, you said two straight sentences with proper grammar! I am...I am...so surprised," said Peter as his adrenaline gained momentum. He briefly flapped his hands but then stopped very quickly.

Frank stepped toward Peter to lightly slap his head, but Peter very calmly moved out of the way. Several other kids were impressed by this action—or the lack of action on Peter's part. Frank then attempted to punch Peter hard in the arm, but Peter executed the blocking technique perfectly, just as Sammy had taught him.

By now, the cafeteria monitor, a lady most of the kids called Cruella, began making her way toward the action. However, she figured it was *Peter* who was once again up to no good.

As a stunned Frank got ready to swing at Peter again, his two buddies, Jim and Tony, grabbed Peter so Frank could get a shot in.

Peter, who was unfairly unmanned, began to panic. *The social story didn't prepare me for this!* Just then, Freddy ran over, and in a rush of adrenaline, grabbed the pressure points of Jim and Tony's wrists and yanked them forcefully in opposite directions. They let go and Freddy shoved them away. This enabled Peter to execute one more very nice block against Frank O'Day, who then lost his balance and fell to the floor. Out of breath, Peter gasped. "You're not as tough as you thought."

Frank was stunned! Just then, Ms. Cruella came over and pointed accusingly at Peter and Freddy.

"You two go to the principal's office. You"—she pointed only at Peter—"are not going to be able to stay at this school if you keep causing trouble like this!"

Suddenly, another voice interjected into the commotion. "These two are not in trouble!" Peter knew that voice; it was his wonderful resource teacher, Ms. Jones! "Peter acted completely in self-defense and did not throw a single punch. His friend only got involved when Peter was being held by these two young men. Frank threw two punches, and Peter and his friend did not throw a single punch!"

The other kids watching echoed that sentiment. "You three," boomed Ms. Jones, pointing at Frank and his friends, "are the ones going to the principal's office. Come with me now!"

ooooo

Peggy Jones had skipped her lunch and secretly watched what was going on in the cafeteria. She had decided to play detective as Doug had suggested and get to the bottom of this mess. She was now also sure that Mrs. Mathers was in on the conspiracy. However, with Peggy, Freddy, and several other kids as witnesses in the cafeteria, Mathers would have no choice but to discipline Frank O'Day and his friends.

ooooo

Several kids patted Peter on the back and congratulated him. Freddy could not contain his excitement.

"Dude, you were awesome! You put him in his place!"

"I need a sensory break," Peter said and then took the rest of his lunch to the sensory room to calm himself down. He truly was mentally exhausted but thoroughly satisfied.

19

As the four members of the Kid Sqaudron walked home from school, they were all pumped up. Sammy slapped Peter on the back as Freddy explained how awesome Peter had handled himself at lunch. Several other kids came over and congratulated him for putting Frank in his place. One time, Peter responded with "Thank you. I am a Jedi, like my father before me." The other kid stood baffled and all four members of the Kid Squadron said almost in unison, "Return of the Jedi!"

"Well, like I said," said the boy, "nice going." He then darted off, and the four friends talked about what they were going to play on Peter's Xbox.

When they returned home and shared the exciting news with Mrs. Salmons, she hugged Peter fiercely. "I was a nervous wreck all day. I could not believe I was letting you go to school with what's going on! I'm so sorry, but I'm proud of you. You tell me what you want for dinner and when your dad gets home, we'll go."

"I want Anne's Pizzeria," said Peter.

"That's what I figured," said Jennifer.

ooooo

Mathers was frustrated. Her efforts to set up Peter to have temper tantrums in the school setting and ultimately be placed in the alternative school had initially progressed very nicely. Now, after Peter's one-week absence from school, he came back a new kid. Peter had kept his cool in all of his classes and in the lunchroom. He had defended himself flawlessly in the cafeteria against Frank, and even had support from a new friend, Freddy Gorski. What had happened last week? Since Frank had been unable to antagonize Peter, Frank had been the one to lose his cool. With multiple witnesses and no way to spin this against Peter and Freddy, she had had no choice but to discipline Frank.

That night, she called Steinbeck to report on these developments. After giving her report, she said, "I'm afraid we have no choice but to pull the plug on this scheme. With his mom and dad being so educated and on top of everything, our hands are tied. I mean, his mom has been threatening to sue the district. Even though I was careful to not make any decisions that were illegal, we still can't afford the bad publicity of being sued!"

A clearly exasperated Steinbeck grumbled, "You're probably right. Go ahead and switch back his lunches and reinstate all his accommodations. Let's diffuse him and his parents for now. I've dealt with his feisty mom on several occasions. When the time is right, we'll strike back."

Steinbeck could not believe this. All of his schemes over the years had worked so beautifully. In a major way, he had begun to feel invincible. How the heck could a boy with autism be stopping him like this when he always had everyone else in the community fooled and got his way? No one else, including parents, school board members, other administrators, and even the police, ever had any reason to suspect him. His perfect cover now seemed blown all because of Peter Salmons. This was Steinbeck's district, and Peter would definitely have to pay.

ooooo

John Marsch felt highly stressed out. His tour of duty in Iraq had left him with what shrinks called post-traumatic stress. He had had a criminal background before he had enlisted in the army. Most of his actions as an adolescent had been done to spite his father. His old man had been an army sergeant and had forgotten to turn off that role as a husband and father. The man had expected absolute compliance from his wife and three sons. His discipline methods were often harsh and physical. When eighteen-year-old John had enlisted in the military, the army overlooked his poor psychological test scores and his criminal past because of who his father had been.

After being deployed to Iraq, the rebellious nature kicked in again. Feeling bitter toward his father and the institution that had made him the monster that he was, he once again began breaking rules. Now, he was a former veteran who was moody, paranoid, and a career criminal. Andrew Steinbeck had found him and paid him a huge sum of money to steal and deliver the school equipment. However, since Steinbeck had been spooked by the cops, he had put the operation on hold and wanted his whole team to lie low. Steinbeck said his reason had something to do with an autistic kid discovering his plan and reporting it to the authorities. What were the odds? This lying low was driving John crazy because he always needed to be in the action and loved the thrill of danger and stealing. Another problem was that John was paranoid about the government. If they were onto Steinbeck, then they may be onto him also. He would not and could not let them take him. If necessary, he would use the arsenal of weapons he had obtained from the black market to defend himself. John Marsch would not go quietly.

20

Peter flapped his hands as he played under the sheets after he and his parents returned from Anne's Pizzeria. He was excited about his success in the cafeteria that day. However, there was something else on his mind that was bothering him. There was something the mysterious other guy had said in the hotel, but he was having trouble remembering what it was. This was surprising since he often had a superior memory. He remembered every other part of the conversation except for that one part! The only flaw with Peter's memory of conversations was that he sometimes did not have control over what he remembered or forgot. Earlier at dinner, his parents had told him how proud they were of him and to keep being a trooper at school. That had initially confused him, because he wasn't a trooper. Then he realized that that must have been a figure of speech. As he and his parents had continued to talk, his dad had said, "I'm going to call John Scagglione and tell him how well things went today and that Frank will be suspended." *John Scagglione. John Scagglione. John Scagglione.* That was it! The mysterious other guy had the same first name as the police officer. The guy had said, "Whenever John Marsch receives an assignment, he delivers. So relax, I'll get your items."

For once, his free flight of ideas, which means his mind wandering, worked to his advantage. It had enabled him to connect John Scagglione to John Marsch.

"That's it!" shouted Peter. "That has to be the guy's name." Peter ran downstairs and excitedly told his parents that he remembered what the other guy's name was. "I have to tell the two police officers," said Peter, sounding nervous.

"That's wonderful!" said Jennifer. "However, please tell us what his name is, and *we'll* call the police and tell them. I really don't want you to have to go through the stress of going back to talk to the police."

"Mom, I have to go tell only them. They said, 'If you remember *anything* else, please don't tell anyone else.'"

"I do actually remember the female officer making that comment," said Joe, realizing that Peter was taking this directive very literally and to the extreme. "Son, your mom is right. I know the lady cop said don't tell anyone else, but I'm sure she wouldn't mind if you told us."

"She said 'don't tell anyone else!'"

"Peter, tell us now what the guy's name was!"

"No!"

"It's okay," said Jennifer. "Maybe it's better if Peter goes to the cops and tells them directly. Please call them now. It's only eight, and hopefully there will be someone there to talk to."

ooooo

Christine Jensen worked diligently as the front door of the police station opened up. Here was the autistic boy and his father again! She had known that they were on their way with more important information pertaining to the case. As the mole inside the police station, she was once again prepared to play spy and provide Andrew Steinbeck with useful information. The boy and his father walked up to her to report that they were here. She told them to take a seat and that she would let Scagglione and Madigan know that they were at the station.

Peter looked at her and said, "Oh, you are wearing different earrings. I like these better. You look very beautiful."

Christine chuckled and beamed at this comment. "Wow, you sure are observant, and you are very polite! Yeah, my husband just bought these for me not too long ago. He was actually doing it to get out of the doghouse," said Christine mischievously.

"Doghouse, D-O-G-H-O-U-S-E. It's a compound word. I like spelling words."

"Okay, Peter," said the father. "Let's go sit down and let this kind lady get back to her work. It looks like she's working hard here."

Christine watched as Peter and his dad walked to the bench to wait for the detectives. She felt an unbelievable mixture of emotions in her gut and tried desperately to fight back tears. This boy had just touched her in a way that she hadn't felt loved in a long time. Her husband, Ben, loved her and treated her pretty well, but they both had busy lives. Also, she and Ben had tried to have children but were unable to have them. They had thought about adoption but that also did not work out. Peter had such an innocent and charming personality! It was easy to report on his being onto Steinbeck when he was *just* the boy with autism. Now, she felt a real connection to him. This kid was absolutely amazing the way he remembered her earrings! How could she go through with her duty to Steinbeck now that she had such a feeling of compassion for Peter?

Since her life had become so boring and she felt so lonely because of rarely seeing her husband, she had been easily charmed into going along with Steinbeck's evil schemes. He had approached her at a bar a couple of years ago and sweet-talked her into telling about how she disliked her job at the police station. He then convinced her into being his eyes and ears inside the police department and offered her a lot of money to do this. At least he wasn't hurting anybody, not until now. She was aware of what Steinbeck and the school were trying to do to Peter, and this had made her angry. Yet, she had tried to tell herself that no serious harm would be done.

As she sat there, she overheard Peter and his dad talking.

"I don't want to go in there. Mr. Scagglione is not nice."

"I didn't think he was that great either, Peter," said the father. "Just remember, you are being a good citizen by telling him everything you heard."

"Good citizen," said Peter. "C-I-T-I-Z-E-N."

"That's right, son. Remember, I'll be right there with you. We are in this together."

That was all Christine could take. She stepped away from her desk as tears began pouring down her face. This settled what her next course of action would be. She would not help Steinbeck anymore with hurting this boy and would not tell him about this latest development. In fact, Christine wondered if there was more she could do to help Peter and make amends for her wrongs. How could she have been so evil for so long? Steinbeck and his cronies from the school were monsters for what they were doing! She wanted nothing but to stop Andrew Steinbeck this time! It would be difficult, but she had to figure out how to proceed from here.

21

Joe walked with Peter as John Scagglione and Kim Madigan escorted them into their office. Scagglione had his usual stoic and less than friendly demeanor. As Scagglione had them take a seat, he said, "I certainly hope this information is valuable this time. We've wasted a lot of time staking out Steinbeck's house, and it has cut into our time for working other cases and solving this one."

"Oh, Dad, time to go home. He's mad. I can't do this. I can't do this!"

Joe felt frustrated not only by Scagglione's attitude but by the fact that he and Jennifer hadn't thought to write a social story about how Peter could handle himself at the police station. Anyway, it was too late for that, and it was time to improvise.

"All right, listen!" said Joe firmly to the officers. "I know you are busy and frustrated by the lack of a serious break in the case. I also know it's hard to communicate with my son, who has autism. However, I love him with all my heart. He has more heart than most people and has many special talents. In fact, it's only because of his autism that you have any serious leads at all in this case. Anyway, your tone of voice and demeanor are very intimidating for Peter. My son shuts down and doesn't think quite as clearly when he is stressed out. In fact, Peter wanted to come to you tonight. He refused to tell my wife and me this new information because you two had told him not to tell anyone else if he had something new. He was afraid to go against your orders and he takes orders very literally! Therefore, please be open-minded and change your demeanor and tone significantly if you want Peter to help you."

The two officers sat quietly for just a moment. Joe sensed that Kim seemed pleased that he had put Scagglione in his place. However, Joe expected Scagglione to continue his tough-guy manner and perhaps even ask them to leave the office. At best, Joe figured Scagglione would be sarcastic and use a mocking kind of voice.

Instead, Scagglione seemed genuinely guilty and said, "I apologize for my attitude. Things have indeed been very stressful. Peter, I'm sorry."

"He means it, Dad," said Peter.

"First of all, let me ask this…would you like a Coke or a Pepsi?"

"None of the above," said Peter. "I'll have water. I'm not supposed to have any caseins or glutens. They give me meltdowns. Pop also makes me burp."

After providing Peter with a bottled water, Peter began trying to tell about John Marsch. Peter said, "The other guy said, 'Whenever…receives an assignment, whenever…receives an assignment…" Peter ended up burying his face in his hands. Joe felt that he knew what was going on here. Peter was afraid because the other guy had seemed more dangerous than Steinbeck. Joe was about to intervene, but Scagglione did instead.

"Peter," began Scagglione, "Please don't be scared. You have to tell us what the guy's name is so we can catch him. Tell us his name and you'll be safe from him and Mr. Steinbeck. I will not let *anyone* hurt you."

"You promise?" said Peter.

"I promise."

"Okay, the man said, 'Whenever John Marsch receives an assignment, he delivers. So relax, I'll get your items. Nonetheless, stealing the Revolabs, iPads, and Smart Boards was standard rate.'"

"John Marsch was the guy's name?" asked Scagglione.

"Yeah, he sounded mean and angry. He was scary."

"Peter, you did awesome! We will find this guy and make sure he is stopped!" exclaimed Scagglione.

Peter then added, "Oh, I smelled garlic in the hotel room. It smelled like overcooked garlic bread!"

Joe noticed that John and Kim both looked very excited by this information.

"Thank you so much, Peter," said Scagglione. "That information may be the evidence that ties the other clues together! Mrs. Allen from the administration building reported that there was a strong smell of garlic in the building when she arrived! Thanks again, Peter."

Peter paused before responding and then said, "You're welcome. Oh, one more thing. You need a haircut."

John and Kim both laughed, and then John exclaimed, "Yeah, Liz has been telling me the exact same thing."

"Who is Liz?" asked Peter.

"She is my girlfriend and a very special lady. Thanks again, Peter, and if you think of anything else, please don't be concerned about coming back to tell us anything."

"Also," added Kim, "feel free to tell your parents."

ooooo

John and Kim sat with Chief Emanuel and relayed the new information to him the next morning. Emanuel, who earlier in the week had ended the stakeout on Steinbeck, was hesitant to start another one.

"Well, there does seem to be a connection, especially since Peter noticed the smell of garlic," said Emanuel. "That truly does blow my mind that this kid could smell that through the wall! However, a lot of people eat garlic."

"Chief, there's more," said Kim. "We've already run the name John Marsch through our criminal database. There is a John Marsch with a criminal background that lives twenty miles from Centerville just outside Riverview Park in a cabin in the woods."

This information caused Emanuel's eyebrows to raise.

Kim continued, "He has a history of theft since he was fourteen. Plus, he served in Iraq for two years and was dishonorably discharged for guess what."

"What?" said Emanuel.

"Stealing army equipment from his unit."

"Well," said Emanuel, "this is interesting but…"

"Actually, chief, there's a little more from the file," stated John. "This Marsch character was not stealing the equipment for himself. He was allegedly being paid by an Iraqi terrorist cell to steal the weapons. Therefore, he has returned to the states since being dishonorably discharged from the army. He's worked a few menial jobs but has had trouble keeping them."

"Interesting," said Emanuel, "but why wasn't he executed or at least imprisoned for treason since he was providing weaponry for the enemy?"

"Basically, the file implied that there were some corrupt politics involved with his admission into the army," explained Kim. "It seems as if he was admitted to the army despite a poor score on his psychological test and his criminal history. We think the army probably didn't want this error exposed if they went through with a court marshal treason trial. Therefore, a simple dishonorable discharge was an easy out for both of them."

"I think I see where you are going with this information," said Emanuel. "Still, tell me how this information applies to this case."

Kim added, "Well, the fact that Marsch is a criminal-for-pay. Since we know that someone used an electronic key to enter the district building, we figured at that time that a district employee had not done the actual stealing. Now, we're certain that Marsch must have been paid by Steinbeck to steal the equipment. Everything Peter said corroborates what we know about this John Marsch."

"If it truly is the same, John Marsch"—Emanuel sighed—"well, I understand your logic. Also, the garlic connection does seem to tie all the evidence together, which makes me think that the garlic smell is definitely not a coincidence. Again, I'm just concerned about using money from the police budget to keep going on stakeouts because of the testimony of one child."

"Also don't forget about what Assistant Superintendent Adam Cruthers reported to us yesterday," said John. "That really ties everything together. Consider the whole timeline. First, Steinbeck hires two cronies to serve as key administrators in the school system despite objections from his assistant superintendent and the school board. One of these people, Principal Anne Mathers, has a theft on her record from when she was in college. Years later, Steinbeck hires an unstable war veteran with a criminal history to enter the administration with an electronic key card. This veteran smells of garlic and leaves behind a major smell in the building. Shortly after that, Peter, who has exceptional hearing and memory, hears Steinbeck talking to Marsch and smells the garlic on Marsch. Someone finds out that Peter hears the conversation, Steinbeck finds out and has Mathers and Mr. Shurna implement this conspiracy to pay back Peter. Everything fits, and I'm confident if we follow this Marsch character enough…"

"I know what you're saying and I truly have a headache. It's just that there is so much circumstantial evidence and political ramifications—"

"But, Chief, with all due respect," said John as his anger rose. Emanuel then raised a hand to signal him to hold on.

"However, I will allow you two to stakeout this John Marsch's house. I'm giving you guys three days, and that's it!"

"Three days! Come on, Mr. Emanuel, stakeouts take time and patience…" whined John.

"Three days," boomed Emanuel. "This decision is final and non-negotiable."

22

As Kim Madigan and John Scagglione drove toward John Marsch's last known residence, they entered the less developed part of town and drove on a road through a woodsy area.

"Well, it looks like this guy doesn't want many visitors or attention," said Kim.

"He probably doesn't. Living in isolation is probably necessary because of his lifestyle. I believe this guy is a psycho, so we need to be very careful. We need to park far enough away so he won't spot us."

Kim sighed. "Yeah, we should be careful. You know, I've actually done some more research on this Marsch character. His dad was a sergeant and a very accomplished soldier, especially in the Vietnam War. His name was Nathan Marsch, and he flew multiple rescue missions. He was quite a hero on the battlefield and won numerous medals for his heroics. At the same time, as a sergeant, he was known for having a hot temper and being very hard on his troops."

"Interesting stuff," said John.

"Yes, indeed. In fact, I'm guessing that perhaps Nathan ran his home the same way he ran his platoon in Vietnam. That could explain why young John became so messed up. Anyway, this is frustrating. I hate stakeouts because they rarely produce results. We really need a break in this case and soon."

∞∞∞

John Marsch adjusted his binoculars to get a closer look at the man and woman sitting in the sedan. He noticed that they were watching his house from a distance and he had no doubt that they were cops! He snickered knowing they probably thought they were out of his eyesight. What they didn't know about him was he was well trained and an expert in spotting the enemy. Also, his naturally alert and paranoid personality had developed as a child as he had to often be on the lookout for his aggressive father. The government had come for him, and he had to defend himself. He grabbed his assault rifle and took careful aim at the woman in the car using his telescopic sight. His plan was to first shoot her and then begin firing away with his machine gun. After shooting the woman, he should be able to nail the man pretty easily. In addition to being great at stealing, he was also a very good shot. He had her head clearly in sight and began to pull the trigger. "Say goodnight, sweetie."

∞∞∞

As Kim focused on the house trying to see if anyone was home, she felt a nagging sense of foreboding. Maybe it was a woman's intuition, but she felt like someone was watching her. She had also felt that way when they were staking out Steinbeck's home. Suddenly, she heard footsteps behind the car! Just then, everything happened very fast. She looked in her rearview mirror and saw Allan Huisenga with a gun as he was running and aiming in an upward direction. He quickly fired in the air toward the cabin! As the gun fired and then more gunfire erupted from the house, Allan yelled to the two cops, "Get down!" John and Kim ducked just as gunfire shattered their window.

John Scagglione reacted quickly and drew upon his own military training. He drew out his own gun as he exited the vehicle and fired in the direction of the shooter from the house. Kim, who was more scared than she had ever been, reacted on sheer adrenaline and threw open the door and flew out at lightning speed. John landed on Kim to protect her from the gunshots.

ooooo

Marsch fired multiple shots in the direction of the targets. Amazingly, he had missed the woman! John Marsch never misses! It was all because of that middle-aged man that came running out of nowhere. He must have parked far enough away to avoid detection. It didn't matter though; they had no way of escaping. They were trapped behind the car, and the trees from the woods would provide minimal cover. This was just like old times when he had fired at Arabs in the Iraqi desert!

ooooo

Peter, Betsy, and Sammy were engaged in their gun tag game while they waited for Freddy Gorski to join them on this afternoon. Freddy came running into Sammy's yard yelling, "Guys, something is going on! I heard it on my police scanner. There is a police shooting." Freddy was very into cops and the military, and his parents had gotten him a police scanner for Christmas.

As Peter, Sammy, and Betsy huddled around, Peter recognized the voice of John Scagglione immediately. The man was yelling, "This is Scagglione, Madigan, and Huisenga, and we are under attack by suspect. Heavy machine gunfire. We need backup now!" He then proceeded to blurt out the address as best he could.

"That's John Scagglione and Kim Madigan," said Peter frantically. "We must help them! John Marsch is trying to hurt them!"

ooooo

As Marsch's rifle bullets ravaged the car, Scagglione's military training kicked into high gear. He shouted for Kim to take cover behind the trees, and a frantic Kim complied with bullets nearly missing her. Scagglione spoke into his walky-talky and shouted for backup while periodically raising his arm to take shots at the shooter. Allan covered for him when Scagglione spoke into his walky-talky. He sensed he would have to have a miracle happen, or he, Kim, and Allan would not survive. Scagglione then ditched the walky-talky so he could focus on the gunfight. After a brief pause in the gunfire, John rolled through the gravel road behind the trees and took cover. Allan ran in a semicircle motion and attempted to draw the fire away from them!

"Allan, no!" screamed John. However, it was too late as bullets nailed Allan on one of his knees. Fortunately, he was able to roll out of the way behind a group of trees for shelter.

As Scagglione and Marsch continued trading shots toward each other, Scagglione worried that his ammo may be getting low. They could not continue this duel much longer! He needed a clean view of the shooter and to make it count. His sergeant in boot camp had taught him that if you hunt with one bullet, it is important to obtain a clear shot. He then ran towards a knoll drawing fire away from Kim and Allan. As he climed to the top of the hill giving himself higher ground, the firing from Marsch subsided as the professional criminal desperately tried to relocate his primary target. Sweat poured down Scagglione's brow as he perched himself between two boulders and focused on the window. *Okay, I have to concentrate like Peter Salmons and lock in on this hard-to-focus-on target.* Without any binoculars, Scagglione was at a distinct disadvantage. As a bullet fired and nearly missed him, Scagglione zeroed in and fired his remaining two shots toward the window of the farmhouse. He then heard an agonized scream— the shooter was hit! Sensing that the shooter was away from the window, Scagglione retraced his steps and ran towards Kim, who was now tending to Huisenga.

"Are you okay?" Kim said to Scagglione.

"I'm fine! The question is how is our guardian angel here?"

"I'll be okay," said Allan. "He just grazed the side of my right knee. Now, go in there and finish off that guy!"

Fortunately, Allan had a first-aid kit with him. The two cops found the tourniquet and wrapped up Allan's leg.

John said frantically into the walky-talky, "Officer down, Officer Huisenga is wounded, send the paramedics!"

John then looked at Kim and said, "I'm going in after Marsch! He is hurt but probably still alive. You stay out here with Huisenga and wait for backup."

"Don't stay with me!" bellowed Allan. "You two have a better chance of taking him down together. I was wounded worse in Vietnam. I'll be fine!"

"Since he's not wounded badly, I'm not letting you go in there by yourself!" said a defiant Kim to John. "I'm going in with you."

"Kim," scolded John in protest, but she was already following him toward the house. Plus, he had learned a while back the futility of arguing with the woman.

ooooo

John and Kim kicked open the door of the locked cabin door. The house reeked of garlic and cigarette smoke. The officers approached cautiously with guns drawn and observed the poorly decorated interior design, cobwebs and half-eaten food on the table. Just then Kim suppressed a scream as she noticed quick movement across the living room floor. It was only a rat scattering across this dump.

"He is probably still upstairs," said John in a whisper as they inched toward the bottom of the stairwell.

ooooo

Marsch ditched his machine gun as the shoulder of his shooting hand was badly wounded, so with his other hand, he grabbed a grenade. The two cops were now in his house, but the third one seemed to be out of commission. However, more government officials would certainly be coming soon. In fact, he could hear sirens blazing through the forest.

It was time for John Marsch to go out in a blaze of glory.

"All right, don't come any closer!" yelled Marsch at the top of the stairs. "If I pull the clip of this grenade or drop it, the house blows up! Leave me alone, go away!"

A highly alert John Scagglione calculated his actions. If he shot at the madman, would he have time to catch the grenade? Highly unlikely.

"Put down the grenade, Mr. Marsch," said Scagglione. "You hear the sirens. There is no way out of this for you. No one else has to get hurt."

Marsch, who was practically incoherent now, began rambling about the government and persecution.

Kim was also now on high alert and remembered what she had read about his dad. She figured he had probably been abused by this military dad and decided to go out on a limb and play that card. "Mr. Marsch," said Kim, "what your dad did was wrong. He's the bad guy, not you."

"I'm still going to a military prison!" yelled Marsch.

"If you spare us, a judge and the army will take that into consideration. The state may even go for a lesser sentence. We'll do what we can to get you help and see to it that the truth comes out about your dad. Your dad abused you and needs to be punished."

"Yes, he does. He was an evil jerk!" shouted Marsch.

"Yes, indeed. Help us now, and we can help expose your dad to the public for the jerk he was."

"He needs to be punished!" rambled Marsch.

"That's right, I agree. We'll help you do that. Hurting us or yourself won't bring justice to your dad."

As she was talking to him, she began walking up the stairs. Marsch was now crying and talking more gibberish.

"Please give me the grenade," said Kim.

Marsch hesitated and then resignedly handed over the grenade. He then fell to the floor, completely exhausted, and continued crying.

John Scagglione was still crouched on the floor with his gun aiming at Marsch and his heart beating a mile a minute. His mouth and jaw were wide open and he could not believe what he was witnessing. A few seconds later, the cops arrived and swiftly took control of the situation. They arrested Marsch, and John and Kim made official statements. As Marsch's house was thoroughly searched by the cops, Scagglione looked at his partner with a new level of respect.

"That was pretty impressive, Dr. Freud," he said.

"Hey, I was just putting my bachelor degree in psychology to good use. Funny thing, when I declared my major, many people weren't sure how much it would benefit me in life. Anyways, I guess you're glad I went into that house with you after all."

23

The Kid Squadron cheered as they were huddled around the police scanner and heard the report that Detectives Madigan and Scagglione were safe and Marsch was arrested.

"Thank goodness my friends are safe," yelled Peter.

"You're quite a guy, Peter," said Betsy. "You have friends in high places, dude!"

Peter looked confused, so Betsy explained that he was lucky to have friends who were police officers.

The kids then continued to play gun tag, and they reenacted the operation they'd just heard.

ooooo

A few days later, John and Kim visited Allan Huisenga in the hospital where he was recovering satisfactorily. Kim was the first to speak as she said, "Thank you for saving our lives the other day. If it wasn't for your quick thinking and being at that house, you'd be at our funerals today."

"Well, I may need the fact that I saved your lives in order to save my job. I was illegally following you guys."

"Speaking of that," said Scagglione, "why exactly were you following us?"

"I'm not completely sure. I think I just needed to be part of the action. I've been bitter for so long about not getting the police chief job. Being able to watch out for the two of you made me feel like I was being useful. I am fond of both of you and just had a bad hunch about this case. I have always had a suspicion of Andrew Steinbeck since before the case."

"Yet you didn't tell anyone?" asked John incredulously.

"I never had any evidence, but something always seemed off about the district superintendent. When you guys parked away from his house, I suspected you were watching him."

"Thank you again for keeping us safe," said Kim.

ooooo

With the arrest of John Marsch, several things fell into place. Marsch was receiving psychological counseling for his traumatic life even as he was whisked away by the army to a military prison. The media reported about his life story and exposed his father for his actions toward his family at a young age. Marsch also told about the conspiracy involving Steinbeck and where the stolen equipment was located. The police apprehended the stolen equipment, which was contained in public storage. The storage smelled of garlic because of John Marsch's frequent visits. This further validated Peter's credibility since he remembered smelling the garlic from a distance at the hotel.

Nonetheless, none of this evidence pointed to Andrew Steinbeck. Apparently Steinbeck had covered his tracks very well, and there was no evidence of him purchasing the space at public storage. Even after John and Kim searched Steinbeck's house, they came away with nothing incriminating on him. John commented at that time that "This creep probably pays more for his toothbrush than I make in a month!" The judge would not grant an arrest warrant based on the word of a boy with autism and the word of a mad man! Everyone, including Chief Emanuel, was outraged and felt that this was bogus. Surely, since Peter's word did lead to Marsch, who then corroborated everything that Peter had said, there would be sufficient evidence for a warrant. However, Judge Newton said that even though there did seem to be a connection, he had to uphold the law completely and needed some more credible evidence before going after Steinbeck, who had a clean record.

ooooo

Christine Jensen walked into Centerville Community Church. The guilt she felt over her role in the scandal absolutely overwhelmed her. She found that she couldn't eat, sleep, or function at work. She had been raised as a Christian but hadn't been to church in years. In fact, she actually forgot most of what the church taught. She vaguely remembered that there was something major about Jesus dying on the cross and all people being forgiven for their sins. Would Jesus forgive her for what she had done?

She walked into the pastor's office for their two o'clock-appointment. The pastor, Reverend Pete Thompson, greeted her kindly and asked her to take a seat.

"Hello, Ms. Jensen, please take a seat and tell me what's on your mind."

Christine again tried to fight tears since this man seemed so genuinely compassionate. "Bear with me, I'm not a very religious person."

"Oh, don't worry about that. God is not religious either. He loves all of us despite how we feel about him and what we've done in the past."

"Wow, I need a God like that right now. I'm feeling very guilty."

After a brief pause, Reverend Thompson said, "Our God is a God of second chances."

Christine sighed and felt that now was the time to confess her sins in the presence of this man of God. "Forgive me, father, for I have sinned."

Thompson actually laughed a little and explained that she didn't have to address him like a Catholic priest but told her she could if she wanted to.

"No, I just couldn't remember the proper protocol for confessing to a clergy. My only frame of reference was from how confessions are done on TV shows and movies."

Christine went on to explain about her being a spy for Steinbeck and her entire role in the scandal that nearly caused harm to Peter.

"I actually know Peter and his parents very well," said Thompson. "They are members here at Centerville Community Church."

"Wow, you still don't hate me?" asked Christine.

"When I became a Christian, I received a heart like Jesus Christ's. Although it's not always easy, I try to see people as being made in the image of God and see them the way Jesus sees them. Therefore, Jesus helps me have a compassionate and forgiving heart."

"You know, I really think I'd like to learn more about this Jesus and church thing," said Christine. "But for now, I'd like to know what I should do to make things right for Peter."

"Well, I've been following the case fairly closely," said Thompson. "In fact, there is a roadblock in the case, and I think there may be a way you can help."

ooooo

Andrew Steinbeck sat on his porch on a late balmy Saturday afternoon. He was a lucky man and truly was invincible! It was amazing that even though Peter was so brilliant and heard him at the hotel, the authorities only had John Marsch. Even though things didn't go exactly as Steinbeck had planned, his alternate fallback plan had worked to perfection. John Marsch had become the ultimate fall guy. The guy was a complete lunatic and a mentally unstable man. Just as Steinbeck had planned, the authorities did not act on the information that Marsch had provided them. How could anyone believe a man that was still traumatized by abuse from his father? The only disappointment for Steinbeck was that it didn't seem like he was going to be able to get revenge on Peter. Well, that was a small price for him to pay. He still was going to have a better life than Peter. Plus, at least, he hadn't let the little wiz kid beat him.

∞∞∞

John was ecstatic after he had his conversation with his colleague, Ms. Christine Jensen. She had told him everything from her side of the story and offered to testify in order to help get a warrant for Andrew Steinbeck. John had never interacted much with Christine over the years; she had always seemed very quiet and shy. Her confession was amazing, and she said she would be willing to accept whatever consequence the police department deemed appropriate.

∞∞∞

Judge Warren Newton sighed as he listened to Christine Jensen's testimony. He had little doubt that this Andrew Steinbeck must be guilty and behind this scandal.

"I appreciate your honesty and letting me know about this. This case has had me deeply troubled. As much as I appreciate your story, along with Officer Scagglione, Madigan and this John Marsch, it is still hearsay."

"But, your honor—" bellowed Scagglione who then stopped himself.

"As much as I believe in my heart that there is a high probability that Steinbeck is behind this, the constitution is clear about warrants. If our justice system is to work, it has to be used correctly. Therefore, before I issue a warrant, I must see some evidence directly tying Steinbeck to this crime."

"What about the phone company records showing the phone calls between Mrs. Jensen and Dr. Steinbeck?" asked Kim.

"Still not enough evidence. Dr. Steinbeck could claim that Ms. Jensen was a friend or former girlfriend. This decision is final!"

Reverend Thompson, who was there for moral support for Christine, and Kim, and John all buried their faces in their hands, clearly frustrated by the judge's decision. It looked as if maybe Steinbeck would get off scot-free after all! Everyone present looked frustrated—everyone besides Christine Jensen. She had a very calm look on her face as if she were anticipating the judge saying this.

"Actually, your honor, I would like you to listen to something."

A very intrigued Judge Newton rose his eyebrows as Mrs. Jensen pulled out her cell phone, typed in something, and handed it to him. What Newton heard shocked him and everyone else in the courtroom. It was a voice mail of Steinbeck leaving messages for Mrs. Jensen! Everything Steinbeck said in these messages indicated her keeping her eyes and ears open at the police station and letting him know if Peter came back with more information.

"I've always had a habit of saving voice mail messages," said a satisfied Christine Jensen.

For the first time in most people's memory, Judge Newton actually cracked a smile.

After her confession, things moved very quickly. Judge Newton wrote the arrest warrant for Steinbeck. After listening to the voice mail messages, the cops had enough evidence to arrest Andrew Steinbeck. John and Kim were part of the arresting team. John absolutely relished this opportunity. As they cuffed and read Steinbeck his rights, John threw in his two cents.

"You know, you are quite a low life, trying to harm and intimidate an autistic boy! He outclassed and beat you!"

"This is a travesty!" bellowed Steinbeck. "Everything I do, I do in the best interest of the kids! I must have been framed because I have no idea who this John Marsch is!"

"I supposed that's why his number is in your caller ID," said Kim. "It's over for you, and you should stop while you're ahead!"

"My lawyer is going to have a field day with this," said Steinbeck.

Steinbeck carried on about suing the police department. John put up a hand and said, "Get him out of my face!"

ooooo

The community and school district had a public relations disaster that would certainly take years to dig their way out of. Principal Mathers and ROCKETS Coordinator Jim Shurna resigned shortly after Steinbeck's arrest. Adam Cruthers actually received the superintendent position, and although he didn't quite have the people skills for this role, he vowed to restore dignity to the position and district. Jennifer received her teaching assistant job back and was transferred to a different classroom.

Peter's life continued to improve for he was lauded as a school hero for helping break the biggest crime in the history of Centerville. Frank O'Day knew better than to pick on the cool kid, not just because of his fame, but also because Peter now knew how to stand up for himself. Peter actually was invited to be a guest on *60 Minutes*, but he and his family declined. He was simply being a good citizen and doing what anyone else should have done. However, his unique ability to recognize voices and remember conversations word-for-word made him a credible witness. The prosecution for Andrew Steinbeck wanted Peter to testify, but Jennifer and Joe were uneasy because of the tension of testifying in a courtroom full of people. Plus, being cross-examined by the defense would be very difficult for Peter. Even the best-written social story may not prepare him for many of the curve balls thrown by a seasoned lawyer doing a cross-examination. Therefore, the state was working on simply having an affidavit or written statement about what Peter heard presented at court.

Epilogue

One year later

John and Kim hurried to make it in time to watch their friend, Peter Salmons, participate in the annual spelling bee competition. They hustled into the crowded gymnasium at Centerville Intermediate School and sat down in two saved seats next to Joe, Jennifer, and Peter's friends. Peter had advanced beyond all the preliminary rounds and was now in the finals. They took a deep breath as they could finally enjoy the competition.

Peter fidgeted slightly as Norman Weber read the next spelling word: *Phlegmatic.*

Okay, Peter thought, *I can't make the same careless mistake so many other people would make, which would involve saying "f."* This word contains a digraph, the rest of this word is simple phonics. "Phlegmatic, P-H-L-E-G-M-A-T-I-C."

"That is correct," said Weber as everyone in the crowd cheered.

The next speller was Henry Wu, a very intelligent kid from Centerville Middle School. He, along with fifth grader Jane Potocki, were the other two finalists. Weber read, "Duumvir."

Young Henry straightened his glasses, stood up straight, thought about the word, and recited, "Duumvir, D-U-U-M-V-I-R."

"That is correct," stated Weber as the crowd once again applauded.

Next up was Jane Potocki. She braced herself as Norman Weber read the next word: *bureaucracy.*

A puzzled Jane reflected on the word and asked about the definition. She then began to spell, "B-U-R-A-U-C-R-A-C-Y."

"I'm sorry, that is incorrect," responded Mr. Weber as she took her seat.

ooooo

Jennifer took a deep breath as this competitive spelling bee roared toward its conclusion. These words were so challenging and so many of the students had done an excellent job spelling them. She marveled at how Peter had so far kept his composure amidst such a challenging environment. He did have a koosh ball in his pocket, and she noticed that he seemed to be taking advantage of it. Jennifer just hoped that Peter would have enough to endure this final round. Henry Wu's turn came up and mercifully; he misspelled the word *kaleidoscope.* It was once again Peter's turn. Jennifer noticed her hands shaking like an over flooded engine with the knowledge that even if Peter spelled his next word correctly, Henry Wu would have another chance.

Weber, said to Peter, "The next word is conscientious."

∞∞∞

Oh my gosh, thought Joe, *I highly doubt even I could spell that word! Come on, Peter, take a deep breath. You can do this!*

∞∞∞

Peter forcefully squeezed his koosh ball. This was certainly a long word. Peter felt his heartbeat and breathing accelerate as panic began to nag at him. However, he took a calming breath, said a short prayer, and began to calm down. He then proceeded to block out the crowd, ignore the flickering light in the far corner of the gymnasium, and focus on the task at hand. Ms. Jones and his mom had practiced with him by explaining that he could ask questions about the word. So he asked "What is...the definition?" After Weber answered, he asked about the origin and pronunciation of the word. Although Peter didn't see how this extra information really helped, he simply focused on breaking down this word: "C-O-N-S-C-I-E-N-T-I-O-U-S, conscientious," Peter concluded excitedly.

∞∞∞

When the crowd erupted, Peter's cheering section—which included Mom, Dad, the two cops and his three closest friends—did a standing ovation. Peter, although very exuberant, did have to bury his hands in his face in order to shield himself from all the extra stimulation. Peter now waited anxiously as Henry approached the podium to try and respell his way back into the competition.

ooooo

Henry was asked to spell the word chlorophyll. He knew the definition of the word and felt very confident that he would nail it. However, his slight overconfidence caused him to neglect the last letter *L* in the word. As Weber announced Peter being the new champion, Henry was almost in tears. He had worked so hard to be the champion this year after barely missing the finals the previous year. He knew his family had had to work extra hard to be successful in this country. In a way, he felt he had let them down. However, his heart warmed after his parents came up to the podium and embraced him in a bear hug. His mom counseled, "You did so great and made your family proud. You have nothing to be ashamed about." His parents' love was therapeutic along with the fact that if someone did have to beat him, he was glad it was Peter Salmons.

ooooo

Peter ran down to his entourage and showed them his trophy. Henry Wu made his way to Peter and congratulated him on his victory.

"Man, you were awesome today!" said the seventh grader.

After a momentary pause, Peter said, "Thank you very much." He was about to look to his mom for guidance on what to do next; however, a confident Peter instead extended his hand to shake Henry's hand.

After Henry walked off, John and Kim walked over to Peter. "Man, you're quite the little dictionary," said John as he gave Peter a high five. "I don't think I could have spelled half those words. If I ever need help spelling a word, I'm going to call you."

"Also, call me if you need help solving a case," said Peter, proud of himself for his wise crack. Everyone laughed.

"You know, I really think these spelling bees have gotten tougher since I was a kid," said Kim. "They really challenge these kids today."

"Well, Peter, I think I need to work you a little harder," joked Peggy Jones. "You hesitated too long on some of the words."

After Peter and his friends wandered off to get more punch and cookies, Supt. Adam Cruthers walked over to talk to the Salmons and the two detectives.

"I would, first of all, like to congratulate all of you on Peter's great accomplishment today. Second of all, I would like to personally apologize for my role in Peter's horrible fortune last year in almost getting him placed in the alternative program. I was certainly blind to what several of my colleagues were doing and absent-mindedly went along with things."

Jennifer, who still felt slightly uncomfortable talking about that horrible situation last year, forgave him. "Last year was certainly a stressful time for a lot of people. I think Steinbeck and his friends had blinders over the eyes of most people in the community."

"I just hope the justice system gives him what he deserves," grumbled John Scagglione. "His trial has been going on for a while."

"Yeah, so much for a speedy trial," said Kim.

"Anyway," said Cruthers, "I think Peter has taught all of us a lot of valuable life lessons. I know I have learned a great deal and have become a better person."

The other four adults completely echoed that sentiment.

Joe then went to round up Peter for the special occasion of taking him to Anne's Pizzeria to celebrate his victory. Peter was certainly a hero for many people.

Glossary of Terms

IEP (Individual Education Plan)—This is mandated for all students with disabilities in the United States. It specifies not only goals but also services that must be made available to students.

Affidavit—A written statement with a promise that the contents are true.

Parallel Play—When two people play next to each other but do not interact.

Caseins and glutens—Two families of proteins that are believed to have adverse effects on children with autism.

Warrant—A document issued by a judge giving permission to the police to search a place or arrest a suspect.

Stakeout—When police secretly watch a person, usually at their house, to catch them in a criminal act.

Superintendent—The head administrator in a school district.

Invoice—A document or bill issued by a seller to the buyer specifying the products, quantities, and prices for products or services the seller has provided the buyer.

Fidget—This is a verb referring to when a person is constantly moving. In the special education field, this word is sometimes used as a noun to describe an object, such as a toy, for a child to play with in order to sit still or stay calm.

Taurine tablet—A type of medicine used to help kids with autism.

Post-traumatic stress—This is a term used to refer to someone who has severe anxiety after a horrible experience. This sickness is often diagnosed in soldiers after a war.

Shrink—The way this term is used in this story, it is a slang word used to refer to a psychologist or psychiatrist.

Reflection and Discussion Questions

1. How and why did Peter's character change and develop throughout the story?
2. Describe Joe's character development from Peter's early childhood to the present time. What advice would you have given Joe when Peter was a child?
3. How did John and Kim complement each other?
4. How did Principal Mathers rationalize her inappropriate behavior? Did she have any good points when she justified her actions?
5. Reflect on Peter's friends. What are some ways that kids can be friends to kids with disabilities and other kids who don't fit in? How can kids support and help kids being bullied?
6. What are some healthy practices schools can implement to service students with disabilities? How can schools improve what they are currently doing?
7. What have you learned about autism and special education in general?

Note from the author

I certainly hope you have enjoyed reading my book as much as I did writing it. Autism and Asperger's syndrome are major topics in our society right now as we continue to learn about it at a breath taking rate. I hope you have a deeper understanding of this disability after reading my story. Peter's character is based on my research as well as talking to people with the disability and parents of children with autism. I also based my story from my own personal experiences with these children since I was a teacher of this population. Also, I have a slight disability myself and some of my characteristics fall within the autism spectrum. Nonetheless, keep in mind that not *everything* about Peter is autistic. Peter is an individual and like anyone with a disability, his disorder does not entirely define him as a person. It is just one aspect of his entire identity. One example from my book where I took personal liberty to add a non-autistic characteristic to Peter was with his ability to interpret people's sincerity when they spoke. It is true that people with autism are extra sensitive to things that most people would not notice. Also, as with most people with any disability, when a person is weak in one area (as Peter was with reading facial expressions), they compensate and are extra strong in another area. A major goal of my story is to show that autism and also other disabilities are not always necessarily weaknesses. Often times our disabilities or labels can be strengths and blessings to others. Therefore, in my story, I attempted to promote tolerance and appreciation of autism.

In addition to the autism awareness, I also hope to empower parents to be vigilant with the school system and involved in their kids' educations. In my story, the school district had some major corruption. Again, some of this was based on my own experience. To clarify, I never experienced quite the level of immorality that occurred in this story. I certainly hope and pray that no school district would do some of the things that certain administrators did in District 52. However, I have sometimes noticed that administrations can make decisions that seem to be in reckless disregard for who gets hurt and may have unpleasant consequences for the students. Finally, I also hoped to address the ongoing school issue of bullying. One of my goals in this story was to give students some healthy methods of dealing with bullies and strategies for students who witness bullying.

For more information about autism, you may visit www.autismspeaks.org. There are also other authors who have written about this disability including Temple Grandin (Thinking in Pictures) and Jodi Picoult (House Rules). I am currently in the process of writing my second book.

CPSIA information can be obtained
at www.ICGtesting.com
Printed in the USA
FFOW05n0654230816

9 781632 688781